Andreï Makine

A Hero's Daughter

Translated by Geoffrey Strachan

SCEPTRE

Copyright © 1990 Andreï Makine
French edition © Éditions Robert Laffont, S.A., Paris, 1990
Translation © 2004 Geoffrey Strachan

Originally published in 1990 as *La Fille d'un Héros de l'Union
Soviétique* by Éditions Robert Laffont
First published in Great Britain in 2004 by Hodder and Stoughton
A division of Hodder Headline

A Sceptre Paperback

1 3 5 7 9 10 8 6 4 2

A CIP catalogue record for this title is
available from the British Library

ISBN 0 340 75128 2

Typeset in Sabon by Palimpsest Book Production Limited,
Polmont, Stirlingshire
Printed and bound in Great Britain by
Mackays of Chatham Ltd, Chatham, Kent

Hodder Headline's policy is to use papers that are natural, renewable
and recyclable products and made from wood grown in sustainable forests.
The logging and manufacturing processes are expected to conform to
the environmental regulations of the country of origin.

Hodder and Stoughton Ltd
A division of Hodder Headline
338 Euston Road
London NW1 3BH

Andreï Makine

Born in Siberia in 1957, Andreï Makine sought asylum in France in 1987. Following his arrival in Paris he wrote *A Hero's Daughter*, his first novel, in French, but failed to find a publisher able to believe a Russian could have written a publishable novel in French. He then offered it as a novel 'translated from the Russian by Françoise Bour', and it was published in 1990. It was not until his third novel, *Once Upon a River Love*, that he was published 'untranslated'. With his fourth, *Le Testament Français*, he became the first author to win both of France's top literary prizes, the Prix Goncourt and Prix Médicis. Its translation into English by Geoffrey Strachan also won the Scott Moncrieff Prize. Since then Andreï Makine has published *The Crime of Olga Arbyelina*, *Requiem for the East*, *A Life's Music* and *The Earth and Sky of Jacques Dorme* (to be published in English in 2005).

'Makine has a quite outstanding gift for tiny, resonant details, from the unused winding sheet that is made into wedding clothes to the tacky souvenir that shatters a shop window. It's a slim volume, but appearances are deceptive – this is an enormously powerful work, and succeeds where many historical doorstoppers fail.'
Stephanie Cross, *Daily Mail*

'[Makine's] grasp of history and its impact on the individual confer an epic grandeur on small books that belie their size and read as far larger works . . . he has created a tragic heroine in Olya, whose beauty and talent betray her as cruelly as did her masters.'
Eileen Battersby, *Irish Times*

'Astonishingly mature and accomplished . . . What sets it apart – what sets all Makine's writing apart – is a wonderful and extraordinary ability to give us the very texture of life in a few spare sentences, his awareness of moments of stillness in which some ultimate reality is revealed, moments when you feel, with his characters, "yes, this is truly how it is, this is what matters, this is what lies beyond the hum and bustle and dishonesties of rhetoric and politics".' Allan Massie, *Scotsman*

'Stunningly accomplished . . . the moments of tenderness and beauty amidst the gloom and the frost are exquisite.' Brendan Walsh, *Tablet*

'Geoffrey Strachan's luminous translation produces a text which is also notable for the author's avoidance of sensational sex scenes and graphic violence. When the narrative jolts do occur, they are shocking and unexpected . . . Andreï Makine, like Zola, creates a fictionalised reality, indicting those who abuse their power while claiming to rule on the people's behalf for the common good.' Sarah Crowden, *The Times Literary Supplement*

'Exquisitely translated by Geoffrey Strachan . . . Makine juxtaposes horror and beauty to haunting effect.' Lara Marlowe, *Irish Times*

'A beautifully realised tale . . . palpable and deeply moving.' Deborah Nash, *INK*

'Few authors can have managed to write a first novel that is both epic and personal, yet Makine is one . . . Ivan and Olya exemplify the tragedy of communist Russia, yet Makine's finest achievement is that they are also so sharply and movingly drawn.' *Irish Examiner*

Translator's Note

Andreï Makine was born and brought up in Russia but *A Hero's Daughter*, his first novel to be published, was, like his subsequent novels, written in French. The book is set in Russia and the author includes a number of Russian words in the French text, most of which, with his agreement, I have kept in this English translation. These include: *shapka* (a fur hat or cap, often with earflaps); *dacha* (a country house or cottage, typically used as a second or holiday home); *izba* (a traditional wooden house built of logs).

The text contains a number of references to events and institutions from the years of the Second World War, which for Russia lasted from 1941 to 1945: the *polizei* was a force of Russian collaborators recruited by the occupying German power to assist them; the Panfilova Division (the 316th Rifle Division led by Major General Ivan Panfilov) became celebrated for the heroism of twenty-eight of its soldiers who threw themselves with their grenades in the path of advancing German tanks in the defence of Moscow during the winter of 1941, and prevented them breaking through.

There are also a number of references to institutions and personalities from the Communist era in Russia. A *soviet* was an elected local or national council and also the building it occupied in a town or village. The NKVD (*Narodny Kommissariat Vnutrenikh Del*), the People's Commissariat for Internal Affairs, were the police charged with maintaining political control during the years of Stalin's purges from 1934 to 1946. The KGB (*Komitet Gosudarstvennoi Bezopasnosti*), the Committee of State Security, was created on Stalin's death in 1953, to take over state security with responsibility for external espionage, internal counter-intelligence and internal 'crimes against the state'; its most famous Chairman was Yuri Andropov. A *kolkhoz* was a collective farm, a *kolkhoznik* a member of the farm collective. A *kulak* was the derogatory term for a wealthy peasant, considered to be an enemy of the Soviet regime under Stalin. The *Komsomol* was the Communist Youth organization, the junior branch being the pioneers. 'Iron Felix' was Felix Dzerzhinsky, the founder of the 'Cheka', the forerunner of the NKVD. COMECON, the Council for Mutual Economic Assistance, was an economic association of East European countries during the Soviet era. 'Beriozka' shops were created exclusively to sell goods to foreign visitors, who paid not in roubles but in foreign currency; some of these accepted vouchers from Soviet citizens who worked abroad and could exchange foreign currency for vouchers. Marshal Georgi Konstantinovich Zhukov was army chief-of-staff from 1941 onwards. Geidar Ali Rza Ogly Aliev was a KGB general. A *kommunalka* was a communal flat. The terms *perestroika* (reconstruction, reorganization) and *glasnost* (openness) became watchwords during the period of Mikhail Gorbachev's liberalization of the Soviet regime from 1985 onwards.

I am indebted to a number of people and, in particular, the author, for their advice, assistance and encouragement in the preparation of this translation. To all of them my thanks are due, notably Thompson Bradley, Edward Braun, Amber Burlinson, Ludmilla Checkley, June Elks, Scott Grant, Pierre Sciama, Claire Squires, Simon Strachan, Susan Strachan and, above all, my editor at Sceptre, Carole Welch.

G.S.

One

How fragile and strange everything is here on earth . . .

What his life had depended on was a fragment of tarnished mirror held in the fingers, blue with cold, of a medical orderly, slim as a young girl.

For there he lay, in this vernal meadow churned up by tanks, amid hundreds of greatcoats, all solidified during the night into an icy mass. The jagged ends of shattered beams bristled upwards from a dark crater to the left of them. Close at hand, its wheels sunk into a half-collapsed trench, an anti-tank gun pointed up at the sky.

Before the war, from books, he used to picture battlefields quite differently: soldiers carefully lined up on the fresh grass, as if, before dying, they had all had time to adopt a particular, significant posture, one suggested by death. In this way each corpse would be perceived in the isolation of its own unique encounter with mortality. And each of their faces could be studied, this one with his eyes uplifted towards the clouds, as they drifted slowly away, that one pressing his cheek against the black earth.

Which is why, when he was first skirting that meadow covered with dead, he had noticed nothing. He walked along, painfully heaving his boots out of the ruts on the autumn road, his gaze fixed on the back of the man in front of him, the faded grey greatcoat on which droplets of mist glistened.

Just as they were emerging from a village – skeletons of half-burned *izbas* – a voice in the ranks behind him called out: 'Bugger me! They ain't half got it in for the people!'

Then he took a look at the meadow that stretched away

towards a nearby copse. He saw the muddy grass piled high with grey greatcoats, Russians and Germans, lying there at random, sometimes bundled together, sometimes isolated, face down against the earth. Then something no longer recognizable as a human body, a kind of brownish porridge, wrapped in shreds of damp cloth.

And now he was one of these dead lumps himself. Stretched out there. Trapped in a little puddle of frozen blood beneath his neck, his head lay at an angle to his body that was inconceivable for a living being. His elbows were so violently tensed under his back that he looked as if he were trying to wrench himself up from the ground. The sun was only just glinting on the frost-covered scrub. In the forest, where it bordered on open land, and in the shell craters, the violet shadow of the cold could still be observed.

There were four medical orderlies: three women and a man, who was the driver for the field ambulance into which they loaded the wounded.

The front was receding towards the west. The morning was unbelievably still. In the frozen, sunlit air their voices rang out, clear and remote. 'We must finish before it thaws out, otherwise we'll be up to our knees!' All four of them were dropping with weariness. Their eyes, red from sleepless nights, blinked in the low sun. But they worked effectively and as a team. They treated the wounded, loaded them onto stretchers, and slowly made their way to the van, crunching the lacework of ice, turning over the dead and stumbling in the ruts.

The third year of the war was slipping by. And this spring-time meadow covered in frozen greatcoats lay somewhere in the torn heart of Russia.

Passing close by the soldier, the young orderly hardly paused. She glanced at the puddle of frozen blood, the glassy eyes and the eyelids distended by an explosion and muddied with earth. Dead. With a wound like that no one could survive. She continued on her way, then went back. Averting her gaze from those horrible bulging eyes, she took out his record of service.

'Hey, Manya,' she called out to her comrade, who was tending a wounded man ten paces away from her, 'he's a Hero of the Soviet Union!'

'Wounded?' asked the other one.

'Afraid not . . . Dead.'

She bent over him and began breaking the ice around his hair so as to lift up his head.

'Well then! Come on, Tatyana. Let's carry mine.'

And Manya was already slipping her hands under the armpits of her wounded man, whose head was white with bandages.

But Tatyana, her hands moist and numb, hastily sought out a little fragment of mirror in her pocket, wiped it with a scrap of bandage and held it to the soldier's lips.

In this fragment the blue of the sky appeared. A bush, miraculously intact and covered in crystals. A sparkling spring morning. The glittering quartz of the hoar-frost, the brittle ice, the resonant, sunlit void of the air.

Suddenly the whole icy scene softened, grew warmer, became veiled with a little film of mist. Tatyana jumped to her feet, holding the fragment aloft, as the light cloud of breath rapidly faded, and called out: 'Manya, he's breathing!'

The hospital had been improvised in a two-storeyed school building. The desks were piled high beneath the staircase, the bandages and medicines filled the cupboards, the beds were lined up in the classrooms; it had been made ready in great haste. When he recovered consciousness after four days in a deep coma, what he made out through the whitish veil that shrouded his eyes in a viscous and painful fog was the portrait of Darwin. Below it he made out a map on which could be seen diffuse patches of three colours – red for the Soviet Union, green for the English colonies and purple for those of France. Then the torpor began to be dispelled. Gradually he became aware of the nurses and would feel a burning pain when they changed his dressings.

A week later he was able to exchange a few words with his neighbour, a young lieutenant who had had both legs amputated. This young officer talked a great deal, as if trying to forget, or to keep boredom at bay. Sometimes he would reach out with his hand towards the bottom of his bed, feeling for his missing legs and, getting a grip on himself, would almost jovially and with a certain bravado come out with something the Hero of the Soviet Union had heard before and would hear again from the mouths of soldiers: 'Good God! My legs are blown to buggery but they're still itching. Now that's a miracle of nature!'

It was this lieutenant who had told him the story of the mirror. Occasionally he caught a glimpse of the woman who had saved his life. From time to time she helped to bed down the wounded, or brought lunch round, but most of the time, as before, she was travelling over the fields in the ambulance.

When she came into their ward she often glanced timidly in his direction and, with his eyes half closed, as he felt the pain easing and giving way to periods of relief, he would smile lengthily.

He lay there, smiling, and what occupied his mind was very simple. He was reflecting that he was a Hero of the Soviet Union; he was still alive, his legs and arms were intact; yesterday they had for the first time opened the window to the warm spring air, with a dry, ear-splitting noise of coarse paper being torn; tomorrow he would try to get up, to walk a little and, if he could manage to do so, he would get to know the slim young girl who kept stealing glances at him.

The next day he got up and made his way across the room

towards the door, savouring the bliss of these still clumsy first steps. In the corridor he stopped by the open window and gazed with joyful hunger at the pale haze of the first greenery, the dusty little courtyard where the wounded were exercising, some of them on crutches, others with their arms in slings. He rolled a cigarette, lit it. He was hoping to meet her that very day, catch her eye ('On your feet already, after a wound like that!') and speak to her. He had given it much thought during those long days and long weeks. He would give her a little nod as he inhaled a mouthful of smoke, screw up his eyes and remark carelessly: 'I have a feeling we've met somewhere before . . .' But occasionally it struck him that he should start the conversation quite differently. Yes, begin with the words he had one day heard in a play his class had gone to see. The actor, swathed in his black cloak, had observed to the heroine who was clad in a pale, frothy lace dress: 'So it is to you, Madam, that I owe my life . . .' Words that struck him as splendidly noble.

Abruptly she appeared. Caught off his guard, he hastily rolled a cigarette and screwed up his eyes. He had not even noticed she was running. Her big boots and skirt were spattered with mud, her hair clung to her brow in moist locks. The Chief Medical Officer was coming out of the room next door. He saw her and stopped, as if to say something to her. But she rushed up to him and, with a sob that burst out like a laugh, she exclaimed: 'Lev Mikhailovich! The van . . . It's hit a mine . . . Near the stream . . . The stream's burst its banks . . . I'd already got out to look for the ford . . .'

The Chief Medical Officer was quickly steering her into his office in the teachers' common room. She went on jerkily: 'Tolya tried to drive across the field. It was packed with mines . . . It was such a blaze you couldn't get near it . . . Manya . . . Manya was burned as well . . .'

There was a rapid commotion in the corridor. The nurses came running, their first-aid kits in their hands. The Hero of the Soviet Union leaned out of the window. The Chief Medical Officer rushed across the school-yard, trailing behind him the leg that had been injured in a bombardment. Clearly audible was the throbbing sound from the engine of the van, its slatted sides reinforced by planks of green wood.

They only became acquainted later. They talked and listened to one another with feelings of joy they had never experienced before. Yet what did they have to talk about? Their two villages, one near Smolensk in the west, the other far away to the north in the marshlands of Pskov. A year of famine lived through in their childhood, something that now, in the midst of the war, seemed quite ordinary. A summer long ago spent in a pioneer camp, fixed forever in a yellowed photograph – thirty little urchins with close-cropped heads, caught in a tense, somewhat wary pose beneath a red banner: 'Thank you, Comrade Stalin, for our happy childhood!' He was seated to the right of a robust pioneer who was frowning behind his drum and, like all his comrades, stared spellbound at the camera . . .

One evening they walked out of the school, strolled slowly through the village half destroyed by fire, talking all the time, and stopped beside the very last *izba*. All that was left of it was a blackened carcass, a charred tracery in the cold spring air. Discernible within it was the grey shape of a great stove, covered with half-burned timbers. But all around it on the ground you could already see the blue gleam of new grass. Above a shattered fence the pale branch of an apple tree in bloom glowed timidly in the dusk.

They did not speak. He studied the inside of the *izba*, as if curiously. She stroked the white clusters of apple blossom distractedly. 'That's quite a stove!' he said finally. 'It looks like ours. Ours had a shelf on top just like that.' Then, without more ado, he began talking, his gaze fixed on the *izba*'s charred entrails.

'Where I lived it was summer when the Fritzes came. They occupied the village, took up their quarters. Two days later the partisans attacked in the middle of the night. They blew up the Fritzes' storehouse and killed several of them. But no chance of driving them out ... They weren't well enough armed. They fell back into the forest. In the morning the Germans were furious. They set fire to the village at both ends. Everyone who tried to escape was killed on the spot. Even though there were only women and children left. Plus old men, of course. My mother had the baby with her – that was my brother, Kolka. When she saw what was happening, she pushed me out into the vegetable patch. "Save yourself!" she said. "Run towards the forest!" I started running but I saw the whole village was surrounded. So then I turned back. And they were already coming into our yard. There were three of them with submachine guns. In a little meadow near our *izba* there was a haystack. I thought: "They'll never find me under that!" Then, just as if someone had whispered in my ear, I see a big basket next to the fence. You know, an enormous basket, with two handles. And I dive under it. I don't know how long I stayed in there. The Germans went into the house. And they killed my mother ... She screamed for a long time ... I was so scared I lay there stock still ... then I see them coming out. One of them – I couldn't believe my eyes – he's holding Kolka head downwards by his feet. The poor kid started to yell ... What saved my life then was my fear. If I'd had my wits about me, I'd have gone for them. But I didn't even twig what was happening. At that moment I saw one of them take out a camera and the other one skewers Kolka with his bayonet ... He was posing for a photo, the dirty sod! I stayed under the basket. And that night I ran for it.'

She listened to him without hearing, knowing in advance that his story would contain all the horror that surrounded them, that they encountered at every step. She was silent, remembering the day their van had entered a village recaptured from the Germans. They had begun to tend the wounded. And from somewhere or other a shrivelled, half-dead old woman had appeared like a ghost and wordlessly tugged at her sleeve. Tanya had followed her. The old woman had led her into a barn; there on the rotten straw lay two young girls – both of them killed by a bullet through the head. And it was there, in the dim light, that the peasant woman found her voice. They had been killed by their own countrymen, the Russian *polizei*, who had shot them in the head and violated the still warm bodies as they writhed in their death throes . . .

They remained for some moments without speaking, then took the road back. He lit a cigarette and gave a little laugh, as if he were recalling something funny.

'When they left the yard they passed close by the haystack. I watched them. They stopped and began sticking their bayonets into it. They thought someone was hiding there . . .'

Twenty or thirty years later, when 9 May came round, Tatyana would often be asked this question. 'Tatyana Kuzminichna, how did you come to meet your Hero?' On that particular day the whole varnishing workshop – ten young girls, three older women workers, including herself and the foreman, a bony man in a blue overall caked with varnish – holds a little celebration. They crowd into an office piled high with old papers, out-of-date wall newspapers, pennants celebrating the 'Victors of Socialist Emulation' and hastily begin to eat and drink, proposing toasts in honour of the Victory.

The office door leads out onto the rear courtyard of the furniture factory. They keep it open. After the noxious acetone fumes it is absolute heaven. They can feel the sunny May breeze, still almost unscented, light and airy. In the distance a car can be seen, raising a cloud of dust, as if it were summer. The women produce modest provisions from their bags. With a knowing wink, the foreman removes from a small battered cupboard a filched bottle of alcohol, labelled 'acetone'. They all become animated, lace the alcohol with jam, add a drop of water and drink: 'To the Victory!'

'Tatyana Kuzminichna, how did you meet your Hero?'

And for the tenth time she embarks on the story of the little mirror and the hospital in the school that springtime long ago. They already know how it goes but they listen and are amazed and touched, as if they were hearing it for the first time. Tatyana does not want to go on remembering the village burned from both ends or the old, silent peasant woman leading her towards the barn . . .

'That year, my friends, it was one of those springs . . . One evening we walked to the end of the village. We stopped. The apple trees were all in flower. It was so lovely it took your breath away. What do apple trees care about war? They bloom. And my Hero rolled himself a cigarette and smoked it. Then he screwed up his eyes like this and said . . .'

It seems to her now that they really did have these meetings and long, long evenings together . . . As the years have gone by she has come to believe it. And yet there was only that one evening in the icy spring, the black carcass of the burned-out roof. And a hungry cat sidling warily along beside the fence, staring at them with an air of mystery, as animals and birds do at twilight when they seem to stir things up in people's minds.

They had one more evening together, the last one. Warm, filled with the rustling and chattering of swifts. They had gone down towards the river, had stayed stock still for a long while, not knowing what to say to one another; then, clumsily, they had kissed for the first time.

'Tomorrow, that's it, Tanya . . . I'm returning to my unit . . . I'm going back to the front,' he said in somewhat sombre tones, this time without screwing up his eyes. 'So, listen carefully to what I say. Once the war's over we'll get married and we'll go to my village. There's good land there. But you must just . . .'

He had fallen silent. With lowered eyes she was studying the footprints made by their boots in the soft clay of the bank. Sighing like a child breathless from long weeping, she had said in a subdued voice: 'Doesn't matter about me . . . but you . . .'

In the summer of 1941, when he escaped from the burnt-out village to join the partisans, he was just seventeen. He could still picture the face of the German who had killed little Kolka. It had stayed with him, the way the pitching of a staircase collapsing beneath your feet in the pallid terror of a vivid nightmare stays with you. This face stuck in his memory because of the scar on one cheek, as if bitten from inside, and the sharp stare of the blue eyes. For a long time the notion of an appalling vengeance obsessed him, a personal settling of accounts, the desire to see this man, who had posed for the photograph with the child's body impaled on his bayonet, writhing in terrible torment. He was absolutely convinced he would encounter him again.

Their detachment of partisans had been wiped out. Miraculously, by spending a whole night in the reeds up to his neck in water, he had managed to escape with his life. When he reported to the regional military committee, he had added a year to his age, and two days later had found himself sitting on a hard bench with other boys in battledress, lean and crop-headed, listening to the blunt, clear, very military language of a non-commissioned officer. He was talking about 'tank phobia', explaining that there was no need to be afraid of tanks and that running away as they approached was a sure way to cop it. You had to box clever. And the sergeant had even drawn a tank on the old blackboard, showing its vulnerable points: the caterpillar tracks, the fuel tank . . .

'In a nutshell: if you're scared of tanks, you've no place in the ranks,' the sergeant concluded, highly pleased with his own wit.

Two months later, in November, lying in a frozen trench, his head slightly raised above the frost-hardened clods of earth, Ivan watched a line of tanks emerging from the transparent forest and slowly forming up. Beside him lay his rifle – it was still the ancient model invented by Mossin, a captain in the tsarist army – and two bottles of explosive liquid. For the whole of their section, as they clung to this scrap of frozen earth, there were only seven anti-tank grenades.

Had it been possible to stand up, with the aid of binoculars they could have seen the towers of the Kremlin through the cold fog to the rear of them.

'We're an hour's drive from Moscow,' a soldier had said the previous day.

'Comrade Stalin's in Moscow,' the officer had replied. 'Moscow will not fall.'

Stalin!

And suddenly the temperature rose. For him, for their Country, they were ready to take on the tanks with their bare hands! For Stalin's sake it all made sense: the snow-filled trenches, their own greatcoats that would soon stiffen forever under the grey sky, and the officer's harsh cry as he hurled himself beneath the deafening clatter of the tank tracks, his grenade in his hand, with the pin removed.

Forty years on from that bitterly cold day Ivan will find himself seated in the humid dullness of a dimly lit bar, chatting amid the hubbub from neighbouring tables with two newly encountered comrades. They will already have slipped the contents of one bottle of vodka into their three tankards of beer on the quiet, and embarked on a second, and will be in such good spirits that they don't even feel like arguing. Just listening to the other fellow and agreeing with whatever he has to say.

'So what about them, those men in the Panfilova Division? Were they heroes? Throwing themselves under tanks? Well, they didn't have much choice, for God's sake: "What stands behind us is Moscow," says the political commissar. "No further retreat is possible!" Except that what stood behind us wasn't Moscow. It was a line of machine guns blocking the way, those NKVD bastards. I started there too, Vanya, the same as you. Only I was in signals . . .'

Ivan Dmitrevich will nod his head, embracing the speaker with a vague and almost tender gaze. What's the use of talking about it? And who knows what really happened? 'And yet,' the words form silently in his mind, 'at that moment the thought of a line blocking the way never occurred to me. The lieutenant shouted: "Advance! For Stalin! For our Country!" And, quick as a flash, it all went. No more cold. No more fear. We believed in it . . .'

It was at the battle of Stalingrad that he won the Gold Star of a Hero of the Soviet Union.

And yet he had never seen Stalingrad. Just a streak of black smoke on the horizon, above a dry steppe so boiling hot you could feel the crunch of sand in your mouth. He never saw the Volga, either, only a greyish void in the distance, as if poised above the abyss at the end of the world. Sergeant Mikhalych gestured in the direction of the black smoke on the horizon.

'That's Stalingrad burning. If the Germans cross the Volga the city's a goner. We'll never be able to hold it.'

The sergeant was sitting on an empty shell case, drawing on the last cigarette of his life. Half an hour later, amid the din and dust-storm of the battle, he would emit a gasp and slowly collapse onto his side, clapping his hand to his chest, as if to pluck from it a tiny, jagged sliver of shrapnel.

How had they come to find themselves with their gun on

this high ground between that sparse woodland and a ravine full of brambles? Why had they been left on their own? Who had given the order for them to occupy this position? Had anyone actually given such an order?

The battle had lasted so long that they had become a part of it. They had ceased to feel separate from the heavy shuddering of the 76 millimetre anti-tank gun, the whistling of the bullets, the explosions. Pitching and tossing like ships, the tanks surged across the devastated steppe. In their wake the dark shadows of soldiers were moving about in clouds of dust. The machine gun rattled out from a little trench on the left. After swallowing its shell the gun spat it out again, as if with a 'phew' of relief. Six tanks were already smouldering. The rest of them drew back for a time, then returned, as if magnetically attracted to the hill stuffed with metal. And once again, in a fever of activity, completely deafened, their muscles tensed, the artillerymen became indistinguishable from the gun's frenzied spasms. As they carried up the shells, even stepping over dead men, they had long since lost track of how many of them were left. And they would only become aware that one of their comrades had died when the rhythm of their gruelling task was broken. At intervals Ivan looked behind him and each time saw the red-haired Seryozha sitting comfortably beside some empty ammunition crates. Each time he wanted to yell at him: 'Hey! Sergeï! What the fuck are you doing there?' But just then he would notice that all the seated man had left of his stomach was a bloody mess. And then in the din of the fighting and the racket of gunfire he would forget, would look back again, would again be on the brink of calling out to him and would again see that red stain . . .

What saved them was the first two tanks burning and blocking a direct attack by the Germans. The ravine protected them on the left, the little wood on the right. Or, at least, so they thought. Which is why when, with the sound of tree-trunks smashing, flattening the scrub, a tank loomed up, they did not even have time to be afraid. The tank was firing at will but the person huddled within its stifling entrails had been in too much of a hurry.

The explosion flung Ivan to the ground. He rolled into the trench, groped around in a hole to find the stick grenade's handle, removed the pin and, bending his arm back, hurled it. The earth shook – he did not hear the explosion but felt it in his body. He raised his head above the trench and saw the black smoke and the shadowy figures emerging from the turret. All this amid a deafness that was at once ringing and muffled. No submachine gun to hand. He threw another grenade, the last one . . .

Swathed in the same hushed silence, he left the trench and saw the empty steppe, the smoking tanks, the chaos of ploughed-up land, of corpses and trees torn to shreds. Seated in the shadow of the gun was an aged Siberian, Lagun. Seeing Ivan, he got up, signed with his head, said something and – still in an unreal silence – went over to the machine gunner's little trench. The latter was partly lying on his side, his mouth half open and twisted in such pain that, without hearing it, Ivan could see his cry. On his bloodied hands only the thumbs remained. Lagun began to dress his wounds, bathing his stumps with alcohol and binding them tightly. The machine gunner opened his mouth even wider and rolled over onto his back.

Ivan stumbled round the tank covered in leaves and broken branches and made his way in under the trees. Two ruts left by the tank tracks gleamed darkly vivid in the torn-up grass. He crossed them and headed towards where the shade was deepest.

Even in this copse the forest could be sensed. Midges swirled around in the slender, quivering rays of sunlight. He caught sight of a narrow rivulet brimming with water the colour of tea, dizzyingly limpid. Water spiders skated about on its smooth brilliance. He followed its course and after a few steps found the tiny pool of a spring. He knelt down and drank greedily. His thirst quenched, he raised his head and lost his gaze in the transparent depths. Suddenly he noticed his reflection, the face he had not seen for such a long time – this young face turned slightly blue with the shadow of its first beard, the eyebrows bleached by the sun and devastatingly distant, alien eyes.

'It's me . . .' – the words formed slowly in his head – 'Me, Ivan Demidov . . .' For a long time he contemplated this sombre reflection's features. Then shook himself. It seemed to him that the silence was becoming less dense. Somewhere above him a bird called.

Ivan got up, leaned over again and plunged his flask into the water. 'I'll take it to Lagun, he must be baking back there under his gun.'

From the citation drawn up on the orders of the Supreme Soviet of the Soviet Union he was to learn that they had that day 'contained the enemy's advance in a direction of vital strategic importance' and had 'resisted more than ten attacks by a numerically superior enemy'. In this text the names of Stalingrad and the Volga would be mentioned, neither of which they had ever seen. But how little these words would reflect of what they had lived through and felt! There would be no mention here of Mikhalych and his gasp of pain, nor of Seryozha in his blackened and reddened battledress, nor of smoking tanks amid trees stripped bare and drenched in blood.

There would be no mention, either, of the little pool of fresh water in the wood, reawakening to all the sounds of summer.

Throughout the war he had received only two brief letters from Tatyana. At the end of each of them she wrote: 'My comrades in arms, Lolya and Katya, send you warm greetings.' He kept these letters, wrapped in a scrap of canvas, at the bottom of his knapsack. From time to time he reread them so that he came to know their naïve contents by heart. What he particularly cherished was the handwriting itself and the mere sight of these regulation folded triangles of creased writing paper.

When victory came he was in Czechoslovakia. On 2 May the red flag was hoisted over the Reichstag. On 8 May Keitel, his eye furious behind his monocle, signed the deed of Germany's unconditional surrender. The next day the air resounded with Victory salvoes and the post-war era began.

Yet on 10 May, Hero of the Soviet Union, Guards Staff Sergeant Ivan Demidov, was still seeking out the dark silhouettes of tanks in his sights and urging on his soldiers, yelling his orders in a cracked voice. In Czechoslovakia the Germans did not lay down their arms until the end of May. And, like stray bullets, the death notices kept winging their way back to a Russia which might have expected that after 9 May no one else would die.

Finally this war, too, came to an end.

Two days before demobilization Ivan received a letter. Like all letters written on behalf of someone else, it was a trifle dry and muddled. Furthermore it had taken more than a month to reach him. He read that in April Tatyana had been seriously wounded, had recovered, following an operation, and was currently in hospital in Lvov.

Ivan studied the hastily handwritten note for a long time. 'Seriously wounded . . .' he repeated, feeling something grow tense within him. 'The arm? The leg? Why not spell it out clearly?'

But along with pity he felt something else that he did not want to admit to himself.

He had already exchanged the hundred Austrian schilling gold pieces for roubles, had already breathed the air of this Europe, devastated but still well ordered and comfortable. On his tunic the Gold Star shone, and the deep red enamel of the other two orders and the bluish silver of the medals 'for gallantry' glittered. And, passing through liberated towns, he was aware of the admiring looks of young women throwing bunches of flowers onto the tanks.

He already dreamed of finding himself back in a goods wagon among his demobilized companions, and the sooner the better, amid the acrid smell of tobacco, looking through the wide open sides at the dazzling greenery of summer, running out at halts in search of boiling water. Apart from his pack he had a little wooden coffer reinforced with steel corners. In it a length of heavy moiré material, half a dozen wristwatches found in a ruined shop and, best of all, a big roll of first class leather to make boots from. The mere scent of this leather, with its fine grain, made his head spin. Just imagine putting on creaking boots and strolling down the village street with your medals jingling ... And indeed a comrade from his regiment did invite him to go and settle with him, in the Ukraine. But before that? It would be an idea first to visit those of his nearest and dearest who were still alive, before seeking his fortune in a new place. 'I could find a pretty girl down there, and besides the people there are much wealthier and more generous ...'

Again he read that letter and the same voice whispered to him: 'I promised ... I promised ... Well, so what? We weren't married in church. I did go a bit far, it's true ... But that was what the situation called for! And now what? Have I got to commit myself for the rest of my life? This letter's a riddle. Let the devil make head or tail of it if he can. "Seriously wounded ..." What does that mean? After all, what I need is a wife, not a cripple!'

Very deep within him another voice made itself heard. 'You're pathetic, Hero, that's what you are. All talk. You'd have been a dead duck without her. You'd be rotting away in a communal grave with a Fritz on one side and a Russian on the other ...'

Finally Ivan decided: 'Right! I'll go there. In any case it's practically on my way. I'll do the right thing. I'll go and see her. I'll say thank you to her one more time. I'll explain to her: "Look, this is how it is . . ."' And he decided to think some more about 'this' on the journey.

When he walked into the hospital ward he did not notice her right away. Knowing she was seriously wounded, he pictured her lying there, swathed in bandages, unmoving. It had not occurred to him that the news was two months old.

'There she is, your Tatyana Averina,' said the nurse who showed him in. 'Don't stay too long. The meal's in half an hour. You can go into the little garden.'

Tatyana was standing at the window, her hand hung at her side, holding a book.

'Good day, Tatyana,' he said in rather too jovial a voice, offering her his hand.

She did not stir. Then she put the book down on the windowsill and clumsily offered him her left hand. Her right arm was bandaged. From all the beds curious stares focused on them. They went down into the dusty little garden and sat on a bench with peeling paint.

'So. How's your health? How are you? Tell me,' he said in the same overly cheerful voice.

'What's there to tell? You can see. I was hit just towards the end.'

'Hit, hit you say . . . But that's nothing at all. And there was that nurse talking about a serious wound! I thought you . . .'

He lost his composure and fell silent. She gave him a long look.

'I've got a piece of shrapnel lodged under my fifth rib, Vanya. They don't dare to touch it. The doctor says the shrapnel's of no account – a cobbler's nail. But if they begin fiddling about with it, there's a risk it could make things worse. If they leave it alone maybe it'll give no trouble.'

Ivan seemed to be on the brink of saying something, but simply sighed and began to roll a cigarette.

'So there it is . . . It can't be denied: I'm disabled. The doctor's warned me: I shan't ever be able to lift heavy weights. And no question now of ever having children . . .'

Then, pulling herself up short, for fear that might have sounded to him like an untoward allusion, she continued hastily: 'My left breast's all scarred. It's not a pretty sight. And I'm missing three fingers from my right hand.'

Tight-lipped, he puffed at his cigarette. Both of them were silent. Then, with bitter relief, she finally let fall what she had matured at length during long days of convalescence: 'Look, Ivan, that's how it is . . . Thank you for coming. But what's past is past. What sort of a wife would I be for you now? You'll find a good healthy one. Because, in my case . . . I'm not even allowed to weep. The doctor told me in so many words. For me emotions are even worse than carrying heavy weights – if the splinter pierces it, the heart's finished . . .'

Ivan studied her out of the corner of his eye. She sat there, her head lowered, not taking her eyes off the grey sand of the avenue. Her face looked so serene . . . There was just a little bluish vein throbbing on her temple, where her closely-cropped hair began. Her features were softened and as if lit by an inner light, utterly different from the radiant, rosy-cheeked girls throwing bunches of flowers onto the tanks.

'She's beautiful,' thought Ivan. 'What a tragedy!'

'Now listen! You're wrong to take it like this!' he said at last. 'Why are you so downhearted? You're going to get better. A fine dress and you'll find as many fiancés as you want!'

She flashed a quick look at him, stood up and held out her hand.

'Well, Vanya, it's time for the meal. Once again, thank you for coming . . .'

He went out through the hospital gates, walked down a street, then swiftly retraced his footsteps. 'I'll give her my address,' he thought. 'Then she can write to me. It won't be so hard for her.'

He went back into the hospital and started climbing the stairs.

'Did you forget something?' the caretaker called out to him in a friendly way.

'Yes. That's right. I forgot something.'

Tatyana was not in the ward, nor in the canteen either. He was about to go back downstairs and ask the caretaker. But at that moment he spotted her dressing-gown tucked away in a corner behind a pillar.

She was weeping silently, for fear of the echo between the floors. Behind the pillar a narrow window looked out over the tiny garden and the hospital gates. He went up to her, took her by the shoulders and said to her in muted tones: 'What's going on, Tanya? Look, here's my address, so you can write to me . . .'

She shook her head and murmured with a gulp through her tears: 'No, no, Vanya. There's no point. You don't want me round your neck . . . What use can I be to you?'

She sobbed still more bitterly, just like a child, turned towards him and pressed her brow against the cold metal of his medals. This frailty, these childish tears, suddenly stirred something within him and prompted a surge of joyous gallantry.

'Listen, Tanya,' he asked, shaking her gently by the shoulders, 'when are they going to sign your discharge note?'

'Tomorrow,' she murmured, drunk with tears and misery.

'Right. Well, tomorrow I'm taking you away. We'll go to my home and we'll get married there.'

Again she shook her head. 'What use can I be to you?' But without asking himself whether it was his head or his heart ruling him, he happily barked out a laughing order:

'Silence in the ranks! To your duties, dismiss!'

Then, leaning forward, he whispered in her ear: 'You know, Tanya, I'll love you all the more with your wound!'

His native village, Goritsy, was almost deserted. He saw the charred ruins of the *izbas* standing there and the useless wooden uprights beside abandoned wells. The head of the *kolkhoz*, who had the emaciated face of a saint on an icon, welcomed them like his own kin. They walked together to the place where the Demidovs had lived before the war.

'Well, there it is, Ivan! It'll have to be rebuilt. For the moment there are only four men here, including yourself. There's a horse of sorts. But that's how it goes. I think we can have a housewarming before autumn comes.'

'The first thing to be done, Stepanych,' said Ivan, gazing at the weathered remains of his father's *izba*, 'is for you to marry us.'

The marriage was celebrated at the *kolkhoz soviet*. Everyone who lived in Goritsy – twelve people in all – was there. The bridal couple were seated, a trifle awkward and solemn, beneath the portrait of Stalin. Everyone drank *samogon*, the rough vodka made in the village. Merrily they cried out: '*Gorko!*' inviting the couple to kiss. Then the women, with voices somewhat out of tune, as if they had lost the habit, began to sing:

> Someone's coming down the hill,
> My lover true, my handsome boy!
> Aye, he's the one, now heart be still,
> Beating madly in my joy!

> He has his khaki tunic on:
> The star shines red, the braid shines gold.
> Why did we meet on life's long road?
> Now tell me why. It must be told.

The dense summer night grew deeper outside the uncurtained windows. Two oil lamps glowed on the table. And the people gathered in that *izba*, far away in the heart of the forest, sang and laughed; and wept too, happy for the young couple, but bitter about their broken lives. Ivan wore his tunic, carefully washed, with all his decorations; Tatyana a white blouse. It was the gift of a tall woman with a swarthy complexion who lived in the ruins of an *izba* at the end of the village.

'This is for you, bride-to-be,' she had said in a harsh voice. 'It's for your wedding. When you came here we thought you were a town girl. We said: "Well, there's one who's landed Ivan, a good catch and a Hero too." Then he told us your story. Go ahead, wear it and be beautiful. I cut it out myself. I knew you'd find it difficult with that hand of yours. My mother was keeping the material for her burial. The borders were all embroidered with crosses. She kept it in a little chest in the cellar. When the Germans burned the village my mother was burned too. No more need for a winding sheet. I poked about in the ashes and found that chest there, still intact! Go ahead, wear it. You'll look lovely in it. It comes with all my heart . . .'

Towards the end of August the frame of the new *izba* could be seen rising up beside the ruins, filling the air with the scent of resin from freshly cut wood. Ivan began covering the roof. From the little shack they were living in they moved into the corner of the *izba* that was now roofed over. In the evening, dropping with exhaustion, they stretched out on sweet-smelling hay scattered over planks of pale timber.

Lying there in the darkness, they stared up through the framework of the roof at late summer stars as they soared and skimmed away in a dazzling dance. All through the village the wispy blue scent from a wood fire in a kitchen garden hung over the earth. The already familiar scratching of a mouse could be heard in one corner. The silence was so intense you could believe you were hearing the shooting stars brushing against the heavens. And in one corner, above a table, you could hear the tick tock of an old chiming clock. Ivan had found it in the ruins, all covered with soot and rust, the hands stopped at a time frighteningly long ago.

Slowly they got used to one another. She no longer trembled when Ivan's calloused hand touched the deep scar on her breast. He did not even notice the scar any more, or her little crippled fist. On one occasion she held onto his hand and drew it over the folds of the wound.

'You see. It's in here, in this little hollow, that it's lodged. The devil take it!'

'Yes. It's bitten deep.'

Ivan drew her to him and whispered in her ear: 'It doesn't matter. You'll make me a son and give him the right breast. The milk's the same . . .'

The *izba* was completed in the autumn. A little before the first snow they harvested the potatoes, planted late, as well as some vegetables.

The snow fell, the village went to sleep. But from time to time they could hear the tinkling of a bucket in the well and the old dog coughing in the yard that belonged to the head of the *kolkhoz*.

In the morning Ivan went to the *soviet*, then to the smithy. Together with the other men he was repairing tools for the farm work in spring. On his return he would sit down at table with Tanya. He blew on a red-hot cracked potato, stole quick glances at his wife, unable to conceal a smile. Everything afforded him a secret joy. It was clean and tranquil in their new *izba*. They could hear the regular sound of the clock. Outside the windows etched with ridges of frost a mauve sun was setting. And close beside him sat his wife who was expecting a child, radiant, a trifle solemn, and more attractive than ever in her sweet and serene seriousness.

After the meal Ivan liked to stroll slowly through the rooms of the *izba*, listening to the creak of the floorboards. He patted the stove's white walls and would often remark: 'You know, Tanyushka, we'll have a whole brood of children. And when we grow old we'll keep warm lying on this stove. It's true, just look at it. It's no mere stove, it's a real ship. The shelf on top is even better than the old one.'

The winter grew severe. The wells froze right down to the bottom. The birds, stricken in mid flight, fell to the ground as little lifeless balls. One day Tanya gathered up one of these birds just outside the house and put it on a bench near the stove. 'It may recover in the warm,' she thought. But the little bird did not stir. The hoar-frost on its feathers simply glistened in fine droplets.

In April they had their son. 'He's so like you, Ivan,' said Vera, the woman with the swarthy complexion. 'He'll be a Hero too.' The child was crying and she had picked him up and handed him to his father.

Towards evening Tanya began to feel breathless. They opened the window to let in the cool April dusk. Vera gave her an infusion to drink but nothing brought her comfort. The nearest doctor lived in a village a dozen miles away. Ivan put on his overcoat and set off at a run on the deeply rutted road. He did not return till the early hours of the morning. He had borne the old doctor on his back the whole way.

The injections and medicines brought Tanya some relief. Ivan and the doctor, both of them light-headed with weariness after their sleepless night, sat down to drink some tea. Vera brought a little crock of goat's milk, warmed it and fed the child.

Before going on his way the doctor downed a small glass of *samogon* and said: 'Now then, if ever her heart falters you must give her this powder. But strictly speaking she shouldn't have had a child, she shouldn't even knead dough . . . Yes, I know, I know, soldier . . . when you're young . . . I was young once myself!' He winked knowingly at Ivan and set off towards the main road.

They called their son Kolka, like Ivan's baby brother who was killed by the Germans.

In the spring, as ill luck would have it, the *kolkhoz*'s only horse died just before ploughing time. Of late they had had nothing to give it but rotten hay and dried stems.

One morning they saw the Party's local boss, the Secretary of the District Committee, arriving in a jolting jeep. No sooner had he jumped down from his vehicle than he pounced on the head of the *kolkhoz*.

'So that's your game is it? Sabotage, you son of a whore? You want to bugger up the entire grain plan for the Region? Well I'm warning you. The perpetrators of deeds like that get shot as enemies of the people!'

He inspected the whole *kolkhoz*, cast an eye over the smithy and the stable. 'Where's the horse?' he demanded. 'What? Dead? I'll bloody well give you: "It's dead"! You're a saboteur!'

They went out into the fields. The Party Secretary continued to fulminate. 'Oh! so he hasn't got enough land for sowing . . . He doesn't stop whinging, this son of a dog. And there, what's that? Isn't that land? Left in your hands, you filthy *kulak*, land like this is land gone to waste.'

They had stopped beside a muddy field that ran down to the river. It was strewn with large white boulders. 'Why don't you clear away those stones?' the Secretary yelled again. 'Well? I'm talking to you.'

The head of the *kolkhoz*, who up to that moment had not opened his mouth, absently tucked the empty sleeve of his tunic into his belt with his remaining hand. In a hoarse voice he said: 'Those are not stones, Comrade Secretary . . .'

'So what are they, then?' yelled the other. 'I suppose they're sugar beet that grew there all by themselves?'

They went closer. Then they saw that the white stones were human skulls.

'That's where our men tried to break through the ring of enemy troops,' said the head of the *kolkhoz* in a dull voice. 'They were caught in crossfire . . .'

Choking with fury, the Party Secretary hissed: 'All you can do is give me stories. You're a pretty bunch of Heroes here in this neck of the woods. You're sheltering behind your past exploits, the lot of you!'

Ashen-faced, Ivan advanced on him, grasped him by the lapel of his black leather jacket and shouted in his face: 'You filthy scum! At the front I shot down bastards like you with my submachine gun. Would you just like to repeat what you said about Heroes . . . ?'

The Party Secretary gave a shrill cry, wrenched himself free from Ivan and flung himself into the jeep. He leaned out of the window and shouted above the sound of the engine: 'You watch out, head man! You'll answer for the plan with your life. And as for you, Hero, I'll catch up with you.'

The vehicle made the spring mud fly as it bounced along over the ruts.

They went back to the village in silence. The cool, acrid smell of humus wafted across from the forest where the snow had melted. The first plants were already appearing on the little hills. As they parted, the head of the *kolkhoz* said to Ivan: 'Vanya, you were wrong to give him a shaking. You know what they say, don't touch shit and it won't stink. In any case, what we have to do tomorrow is start ploughing. And not on account of that idiot's orders . . .'

The next day Ivan was making his way forwards, leaning on the plough, stumbling over the ruts, slithering on the glistening clods of earth. With the aid of ropes fixed to the draught beam, the plough was being drawn along by two women. On the right walked Vera, in big sagging boots that looked like elephants' feet on account of the mud. On the left, Ivan's childhood friend, Lida. She still wore her schoolgirl's skirt, which left her knees bare.

The morning was limpid and sunny. Busily the crows were taking off and settling again on the ploughed land. Fluttering past, hesitant and fragile, the first butterfly shone in a brief, yellow flurry.

Ivan kept his eyes on the backs and feet of the two women as they struggled forwards. Sometimes the ploughshare dug in too deeply. The women braced themselves against the ropes; then Ivan manipulated the handles of the plough, trying to help them. The steel ploughshare sliced through the earth, wrenched itself free and they continued their walk. And again Ivan saw the elephants' feet and the jackets discoloured by the sun and rain. 'The war . . .' he thought. 'Everything stems from there . . . Take Lidka, hardly married and her husband sent to the front. Straight into the front line, into the mincing machine. A month later the death notice and there she is, a widow. A widow at eighteen. What a crying shame! And look how much she's aged! You'd scarcely recognize her. And those varicose veins! Like dark strings on her legs. She used to sing so well. The old folk would climb down off their stoves to listen to her, whilst we, young idiots, used to fight like cocks over her . . .'

They stopped at the end of the furrow and straightened themselves up. 'Take a rest, girls,' said Ivan. 'We'll have lunch.' They sat down on the ground, on last year's dry, brittle grass, unwrapped their sparse meal from a cloth. Unhurriedly they began to eat.

Spring had come. What lay in wait for them was the great drought of 1946.

*   *   *

By the month of May they had already reached the stage of boiling up the half-wild orache plants that grew by the roadsides, tossing in a little scrap of rancid bacon and eating this brew in an attempt to cheat their hunger.

In June the burning wind of the steppes started blowing. The new grass began to shrivel and the leaves to fall. The sun scorched the young corn to a cinder, dried up streams, struck down the starving people who came out into the fields. Even the wild strawberries that could be found at the edge of the forest had hardened into bitter, dry little balls.

At Goritsy one of the peasants arranged with the head of the *kolkhoz* to go and see what was happening in the neighbouring villages. He returned five days later gaunt, with staring eyes, and very quietly, as if he were afraid of his own voice, and constantly looking over his shoulder, began to tell his story: 'At Bor there are only two men still alive. At Valyaevka there's not a soul in sight. No one to dig graves: the dead just stay in their *izbas* . . . It fair gives you the jitters to go into one. Every time you push open a door it's a nightmare. I met a peasant on the high road yesterday. He was heading for the city. The hunger drove him to it. He told me where he came from they were eating the dead, like they did on the Volga in the twenties . . .'

Ivan had become afraid to look at his wife of late. She hardly got up any more. Lying there with the baby, dipping her finger into a brew of orache and old crusts, she tried to feed him. Her face was marked with dry brown spots; dark rings burned round her eyes. Kolka hardly moved on her breast. He no longer even cried, simply uttering tiny moans, like an adult. Ivan himself had great difficulty in standing upright. At length he woke up one day at the crack of dawn and reflected with mortal clarity, 'If I don't find anything to eat all three of us will die.'

He kissed his wife, put two gold watches, the spoils of

30

war, into his tunic pocket, hoping to be able to trade them for bread. And set out towards the main road.

The village was dead. The noontide furnace. Dry, dusty silence. Not a living soul. Nothing but music blaring out from the black loudspeaker above the door of the *soviet*. The radio had been installed by the Secretary of the District Committee, who had ordered that it should be switched on as often as possible, 'to raise the political consciousness of the *kolkhozniks*'. But now the radio was simply blaring because there was no one to turn it off.

And from dawn till dusk, delirious with hunger and hugging the tiny body of her child with his great head, Tatyana listened to rousing marches and the commentator's voice almost bursting with glee. He was reporting on the industrial achievements of the Soviets. Then, the same voice, but now in harsh, metallic tones, delivered stinging critiques of all those enemies who had perverted Marxism and lambasted the agents of imperialism.

In the stifling heat of noon that day, the last before her long collapse, Tatyana heard the song currently in vogue that was played every day. The flies buzzed against the windowpanes, the village was mute, poleaxed by the sun, and this song rippled out, as sweet and tender as Turkish delight:

> All the world turns blue and green about us,
> Nightingales at every window sing.
> There's never love without a touch of sadness . . .

Ivan walked along, taking great strides. In his old knapsack he carried two loaves of black bread, a paper bag containing millet, twelve onions and a piece of bacon wrapped in a scrap of cloth. But most precious of all, the litre of milk, that had long since turned sour, he carried in his hands. 'With this we can feed the lad and then we'll see . . .' he thought.

A dense, dry heat hovered over the fields, like the exhalation from the mouth of an oven. A burning copper sun was plunging down behind the forest but scarcely any evening cool could be felt.

He passed through the deserted village flooded with the violet light of the sunset. The radio above the *soviet* was still blaring away.

As he crossed the threshold he had a premonition of disaster. He called out to his wife. All that could be heard was the incessant buzzing of the flies. A fine golden ray of light pierced the gloom of the *izba*. Ivan rushed into the bedroom. Tatyana lay there on the bed, the child in her arms, and appeared to be asleep. He lifted the cover in haste and pressed his ear to her breast. Beneath the rough scar he heard her heart beating faintly. He heaved a sigh of relief. 'Thank goodness! I've arrived in time . . .' Then he touched the child. The cold, rigid little body already had a waxen sheen to it. Outside the window the sweet voice was unflaggingly pouring out these words:

> All the world turns blue and green about us,
> In the forest gaily purls the stream.
> There's never love without a touch of sadness . . .

Ivan bounded out of the house and ran over to the *soviet*. Blinded with tears, he began flinging stones at the black disk of the loudspeaker, without managing to hit it. Struck at last, the loudspeaker screeched and fell silent. A vertiginous stillness ensued. Only, somewhere at the edge of the forest, like a well-oiled machine, the cuckoo flung out its insistent, plaintive call.

The next day Tatyana was able to get up. She went out onto the doorstep and saw Ivan driving nails into the little coffin's pine planks.

After burying their son and gathering together their meagre luggage, they took the road to the station. Ivan had heard that in the small town of Borissov, some sixty miles from Moscow, they were recruiting drivers for the construction of a hydro-electric centre and providing them with accommodation.

That was how they came to settle in the Moscow region. Ivan found himself at the wheel of an old lorry, whose side panels bore the inscription in flaking paint: 'Next stop: Berlin!' Tatyana went to work at the furniture factory.

And the days, months and years followed one another, calmly and uneventfully. Ivan and Tanya were content to see their lives taking this ordinary, peaceful course. The same as everyone else, that of decent people. They had been given a room in a communal flat. There were already two families living there, the Fedotovs and the Fyodorovs. And in the little room next to the kitchen lived Sofia Abramovna.

The Fedotovs, still a young couple, had three sons, whom the father beat frequently and conscientiously. When their parents were out at work these rascals would take their father's heavy bicycle down from the wall. With a hellish din, running over the other tenants' shoes, they careered up and down the long, dark corridor, where there hovered a persistent and bitter smell of stale borsch.

The Fyodorovs were almost twice as old as the Fedotovs. Their son had been killed just before the end of the war and the mother lived in the hope that the death notice had been sent by mistake: there are so many Fyodorovs in Russia! Secretly she hoped he had been taken prisoner and that some day or other he would return. Fyodorov, the father, had himself been in the war from the first day to the last and was under no illusions. Sometimes, when he had been drinking and could stand it no longer, exasperated by his wife's daily expectation, he would bawl right through the flat: 'Oh yes, you can count on it, he's going to come back. But if he's discharged from the prisoner-of-war camp he's not going to come back here to you. He'll be sent beyond the Urals – or even further!'

Sofia Abramovna belonged to the old Moscow intelligentsia. In the thirties she had been sent to a camp and had only been released in '46, subject to a ban on living in Moscow and some hundred other cities. During her ten years in the camp she had lived through what human language was incapable of expressing. But her neighbours guessed it. When a quarrel broke out in the kitchen Sofia did not try to stand on the sidelines but lost her temper, cursed and swore, using surprising language. Sometimes she hurled turns of phrase at her adversaries that were contemptuous in their exaggerated politeness: 'I give you my most humble thanks, citizen Fyodorov. You are the very pinnacle of courtesy.' On other occasions she would suddenly come out with expressions she had picked up in the camps. 'Listen, Fedotov, you keep your damned thieving hands off the stash in my sideboard. You're wasting your time giving it a spin. There's no alcohol in there.'

But even at the height of these neighbourly quarrels Sofia's eyes were always staring into space to such an extent that it was clear to everyone: she was still back there beyond the Urals. Which was why arguing with her was not very rewarding.

Whether they liked it or not, the Demidovs used to find themselves drawn into these conflicts. But their role was generally confined to acting as conciliators between the Fyodorovs and the Fedotovs when they squabbled, and calming the wives as they sobbed noisily.

Life would have been somewhat lacking in savour for all of them without these altercations. For three days after a quarrel the neighbours would sidle, glowering, past one another, without exchanging greetings. Then they would make it up around a communal table and, after drinking a few vodkas, would begin to embrace, swearing eternal friendship and abjectly begging one another's forgiveness with tears in their eyes. The Fedotovs had an old wind-up gramophone. They would bring it down into the courtyard, put it on a small stool and all the inhabitants of their little building would gather in the mauve dusk of spring. They would shuffle about to the sound of a languid tango, forgetting for an hour or two the morning queues outside the communal toilets, the squabbles over the disappearance of a piece of soap, forgetting everything that made up their lives.

The Demidovs enjoyed these evenings. Tanya would put on her white wedding blouse, Ivan threw a jacket over his shoulders with all his medals in a row. And they danced together, smiling at one another, letting themselves be carried away by the sweet dreaminess of the words:

> Do you remember how we whispered,
> On those summer nights so blue,
> Words of tenderness and passion
> O my dearest lover true . . . ?

The years rolled by at once slowly and rapidly. Imperceptibly the Fedotov sons had grown up, developed into hefty young men with bass voices. They had all married and left in one direction or another.

Some records had had their day, others came into vogue. And now it was the younger generation who played them on their windowsills, commenting: 'That's Lolita Torrez . . . Oh, this one's Yves Montand.'

The only event that stuck in Ivan's memory during those years was the death of Stalin. And, in fact, not the death itself, because on that day they had drunk and wept buckets and that was all. No, it was another day, already under Khrushchev, when they removed the statue of Stalin. Why did they choose him, specifically him, Demidov, for this task? Was it because he was a Hero of the Soviet Union? The head of the vehicle pool had called him in. Ivan found himself among the local Party bosses. They explained to him what it was all about. He had to take his Zis lorry that night and put in some overtime.

This was how the memory of that spring night had stayed with him. They worked in darkness, simply lighting the monument with their vehicle headlamps. A fine rain was falling that had the bitter smell of poplar shoots. The cast-iron statue of the Great Leader glistened like rubber. The pulley on the crane began to do its work: Stalin found himself hanging in mid-air, somewhat askew, gently swaying, staring hard at the people scurrying about beneath him. And already the workmen were tugging him by his feet towards the Zis's open side panel. The foreman of the team, close beside Ivan, grunted: 'Sometimes we were lying there on our bellies at the front and they were chucking so much at us you couldn't even lift your head up from the ground. The stuff was whistling over. A hail of bullets like a shower. Then the political commissar jumps to his feet with his little revolver, you know, like those kids' pistols. And once he yells: "For our Country, for Stalin, forward!" . . . then it grabbed us, you know, God damn it! Up we jumped and went over the top . . . All right, lads! Steer the head towards the corner. Otherwise it won't fit in. Steady she goes . . .'

A fresh breeze could be sensed in the air, with something sparkling and joyful about it. In Moscow, it appeared, passions were being unleashed. Things were coming to the boil in kitchens at the highest level. Ivan even acquired a taste for reading newspapers, which he had never looked at before. All about them everything was relaxing, gaining a new lease of life. An endless procession of Fidel Castros, bearded and smiling, marched through the newspapers, as well as drawings of Blacks with great white teeth, smashing the chains of colonialism, and the engaging faces of Belka and Strelka, the pioneer dog cosmonauts. All this added savour to life and caused joyful hopes to be reborn. As he sat behind the wheel, Ivan often hummed the song that could be heard everywhere:

Cuba, my love,
Isle of purple dawn . . .

And it seemed as if both Fidel and the Blacks on the posters breaking free from colonialism were intimately linked to the life of Borissov, to their own existence. It seemed as if the world was about to be shaken and an endless festival would begin, here and everywhere on earth.

To crown it all Gagarin had taken off into space. And at the Party Congress Khrushchev made the pledge: 'We shall build communism in twenty years.'

At the end of this happy year two important events had occurred in the Demidov family. In November they had had a daughter and just before the new year they had bought a Zaria television set.

At the maternity ward the doctor said to Ivan: 'Now listen, Ivan Dmitrich, you may well be a Hero here, all the town knows you. But I'm going to speak frankly. With a war wound like that no one should have children! Her heart missed a beat three times during the birth . . .'

But it was a time for optimism. They had no thoughts of anything troublesome. On New Year's Eve Ivan and Tanya sat in front of the television, their arms round one another's shoulders, to watch *Carnival Night*, starring the popular actress, Gurchenko, then in the flush of youth and trilling away merrily. They were perfectly happy. In the dim light the dark green glint of a bottle of champagne glowed on the table. The snow crunched under the feet of passers-by outside. From the neighbours' rooms could be heard the hubbub of guests. Behind the wardrobe in a little wooden cradle their newborn was sleeping silently and diligently. They had called her Olya.

In the spring of the following year they were given a flat of their own with two rooms.

* * *

During these years a whole generation who had not known the war came into the world and grew up. Ivan was more and more often invited to the school at Borissov just before the national celebration on 9 May, Victory Day.

Now they addressed him as 'Veteran'. This amused him. To him it seemed as if the war had only just ended and he was still that former Guards staff sergeant, recently demobilized.

At the entrance to the school he was met by a young teacher, who greeted him with a radiant smile and led him into the classroom. He followed her in, his medals tinkling on his chest, and thought: 'How quickly time passes! The truth is I really am a Veteran now. She's young enough to be my daughter and she's a teacher already!'

As he entered the noisy classroom silence fell. The pupils stood up, exchanging glances, whispering, staring at his decorations. They were impressed by the Gold Star of the Hero of the Soviet Union. A Hero. You don't meet one of those every day!

Then the teacher made some appropriate remarks about the great national celebration, and the twenty million lives sacrificed for the sake of the radiant future of these pupils, distracted as they were by the May sunlight, taking as her text: 'No one is forgotten, nothing is forgotten.' After that her voice adopted a warmer, less official tone and she addressed Ivan, who was standing somewhat stiffly behind the table: 'Honoured Ivan Dmitrevich, on your chest shines our country's highest award, the Gold Star of a Hero of the Soviet Union. We should like to hear about the part you played in the war, your achievements in battle and your heroic contribution to the Victory.'

And Ivan cleared his throat and began his story. He already knew by heart what he would tell them. Once he had started receiving invitations he had grasped what he had to say so that the class remained attentive for the regulation forty minutes, much to the delight of the young teacher. He even knew that at the end of his talk – after which there would be a tense silence for several seconds – she would rise nimbly to her feet and pronounce the expected words: 'Now then, children, put your questions to Ivan Dmitrevich.' Once again there would be an embarrassing silence. But in obedience to a look from the teacher, a radiant girl would stand up in the front row, wearing a smock as white as whipped cream, who would say, as if she were reciting a lesson: 'Honoured Ivan Dmitrevich, please will you tell us what qualities of character you valued most in your wartime comrades?'

After the reply, to which no one paid much attention, the most presentable boy would stand up and ask Ivan, in the same conscientious tones, what advice he would give to future defenders of their Country?

At the end of this patriotico-military demonstration there would often be an unexpected diversion. Urged on by the whispers of his fellows, a great scruffy youth would rise to his feet in the back row. And without any preliminaries would stammer out: 'So how thick was the armour on the German Tigers? Thicker or thinner than on our T-34?' 'The gun. Ask him about the gun . . .' his neighbours prompted him. But the boy, bright red, was already collapsing onto his chair, proud of his excellent question. Ivan answered him. Then the bell rang and the much relieved teacher congratulated the Veteran once more and gave him three red carnations, taken from a vase that stood on the desk. Impatiently the whole class jumped to their feet.

On the way home Ivan Dmitrevich always had a few confused regrets. Each time he wished he had told them about a small detail: the wood he went into after the battle and the spring water that had reflected his face back at him.

Journalists sometimes came to see him as well, most often for the anniversary of the start of the battle of Stalingrad. The first time, responding to a question about the battle, he began to talk about everything: Mikhalych, who would never

39

know his grandchildren; Seryozha, who looked so serene, so carefree in death; the machine gunner who had only one digit left on each hand. But the journalist, adroitly seizing the moment when Ivan was drawing breath, interrupted him: 'So, Ivan Dmitrevich, what impression did the "Heroic City on the Volga" make on you in that year of fire 1942?' Ivan was disconcerted. Admit that he had never seen Stalingrad, never fought in the streets there? 'All Stalingrad was burning,' Ivan replied evasively.

After that he got used to this innocent untruth, which suited the journalists very well, for at that time Stalin was coming back into fashion and 'Stalingrad' had a good ring to it. Sometimes Ivan was surprised to realize that even he was increasingly forgetful of the war. He could no longer distinguish between his old memories and the well-worn tales told to the schoolchildren and the interviews given to journalists. And when one day he was speaking of a detail that fascinated the boys: 'Oh yes, our 76 millimetre gun was powerful but it couldn't pierce the Tiger tank's frontal armour . . .' he would think: 'But was it really like that? Maybe it's something I read in Marshal Zhukov's memoirs . . .'

The Demidovs' daughter, Olya, was growing up and going to school. She already knew the ancient story of the little mirror. To her it seemed legendary and alarming – her father lying in a frozen field, his head all bloody; her mother, whom she could not manage even to picture, choosing him from amongst hundreds of soldiers lying all around. She knew that once upon a time there had been a battle, for which he had received his Star – thanks to which he could buy train tickets without having to queue.

They had also told her about her mother's injury, which meant she was not supposed to carry heavy loads. But this did not stop her mother lugging heavy wooden panels about and Olya's father used to scold her for her lack of concern.

When Olya took her entrance exams for the Maurice Thorez Institute of Foreign Languages she experienced the reality of this legendary wartime past in a quite specific way. The friend with whom she had come to Moscow said to her with ill-concealed jealousy: 'You're bound to pass, of course. They'll take you just because of your civil status. It's a foregone conclusion. You're the daughter of a Hero of the Soviet Union . . .'

Two

During the summer of 1980 Moscow was unrecognizable. People who lived in the rest of the country were not allowed into the capital. Most of the children were sent off to pioneer camps. Long before the summer a serious purge had been carried out, in which all 'anti-social elements' had been expelled. There was no sign now of queues in the shops, nor of jostling on the buses, nor of the glum throng of people from the provinces coming in with their big bags to do their shopping.

The cupolas of ancient churches had been hastily white-washed and members of the militia had been taught to smile and say a few words in English.

And the Moscow Olympic Games began. Everywhere coaches could be seen coming and going, carrying the athletes to the events, while foreign tourists idly called out to one another in the deserted streets, busying themselves with guides and interpreters.

From this summer, from these Games, from this influx of foreigners, everyone expected something extraordinary, a breath of fresh air, some kind of upheaval, almost a revolution. For the space of a few weeks Brezhnev's Moscow, like a vast, spongy slab of floating ice at the time of the spring floods, nestled up to this colourful Western life, grinding its grey sides against it, and then drifted off bombastically on its way. The revolution did not take place.

Olya Demidova was totally caught up in this Olympic bustle, allowing herself to fall into a frenzy of happy exhilaration. She had completed her third year at the Institute and had reached that stage in English and French where you are suddenly seized with an irresistible desire to converse. She already spoke with the hesitant freedom of a child that is just learning to run and enjoying the ability to keep its balance.

The interpreters hardly slept now. But their youth and their feverish excitement kept them on their feet. It was such fun in the morning to leap onto the platform of a coach, to see the athletes' young faces, to respond to their jokes and then to go flying through Moscow's resonant streets. In the evening the atmosphere was quite different. Inside the bus, heated up during the day by the burning sun, there hovered the acrid smell of Western deodorants and muscular male bodies exhausted by their efforts. The streets slipped past and the cool twilight of evening swept in at the windows of the coach. The men, slumped in their seats, exchanged idle remarks.

Sitting next to the driver on a seat that swivelled round, Olya glanced at them from time to time. They made her think of gladiators, resting after the fight.

One of them, Jean-Claude, a typically Mediterranean young man (she was working with a French team), sat there with his head thrown back and his eyes half closed. She guessed he was watching her through lowered eyelids. He smiled as he watched her and when the coach stopped at the Olympic Village he was the last to get off. Olya stood beside the coach door, taking leave of the athletes and wishing each of them a good night. Jean-Claude shook her hand and remarked carelessly, but loud enough for this to be heard by the minder who escorted them: 'I've got something that needs translating. Could you help me? It's urgent.'

Olya found herself in his room, surrounded by all those beautiful coveted objects that for her symbolized the Western world. She understood at once that the translation was only a pretext and that something was going to happen which, only a short time before, had still seemed unthinkable. To quell her fear she repeated like an incantation:

'I don't care a fig. It makes no odds. If it happens, it happens . . .'

When Jean-Claude came out of the shower she was already in bed. Stark naked and swathed in a pungent cloud of eau de Cologne, he crossed the room in darkness, and tossed a sports shirt or a terry towel onto the edge of the balustrade. Then he stopped before a tall, dark mirror and, as if lost in thought, ran his fingers several times through his damp hair, on which the blue light of a streetlamp glinted. His skin also shone, with a dark, luminous glow. He closed the door to the balcony, and made his way towards the bed. It felt to Olya as if the ceiling were gently caving in on her in a chamber made of synthetic foam.

After the third night she had just emerged from the building in the early hours of the morning when the man who oversaw the interpreters loomed before her. Without greeting her, he barked: 'So I see you know how to mix business with pleasure! Do I have to drag you out of bed to send you to work? What's going on? Is this the Olympic Games or a brothel? Report to the Organizing Committee. They'll soon sort you out!'

During those three days Olya had been so wildly happy she had not even given a moment's thought to seeking any justification or to preparing a plausible story. On their last night together Jean-Claude was intoxicated with happiness. He had come second and won a silver medal. He drank, talked a lot and looked at her with rather crazed eyes. It all involved a firm he had a contract with and a sports centre, which he would now be able to open. He talked about money without any embarrassment. He became so excited as he talked about all this that Olya said to him, laughing, 'Just listen to you, Jean-Claude, you sound as if you were on drugs!' Pretending to take fright, he put his hand over her mouth, pointing to the radio: 'They're listening to all this.' Then he embraced her and pressed her back onto the pillows. Recovering his breath, immersed in silent exhaustion, he murmured in her ear: 'Yes, I am on drugs . . . you're my drug!'

At the Organizing Committee it all began with shouting. A shrivelled old official of the *Komsomol* with a clammy bald head, dressed in a suit with bulging pockets, methodically tore into their three days of happiness. 'It's not just us you're dragging through the mire,' he yelled. 'You bring shame on the whole country. What are they going to think of the USSR in the West now? Well, what do you suppose? That all the Communist Youth are prostitutes, like you? Is that it? Don't interrupt. And the daughter of a Hero of the Soviet Union, what's more! Your father gave his blood . . . And what if this incident reached the ears of the Central Committee? Have you thought of that? The daughter of a Hero of the Soviet Union! Coming from such stock, to soil yourself like that! Well, we have no intention of covering up for you. Make no mistake about that. They'll kick you out of the Institute and the *Komsomol*. As they say amongst your young friends: "Pleasure has to be paid for." There's no point in crying now. You should have thought of it before.'

After this tirade he removed the stopper from a carafe with a dry creak, poured out a glassful of tepid, yellowish water and drank it with a grimace of disgust. He went over to the window and drummed on the greyish windowsill, waiting for Olya to stop crying. The heat in the office was stifling. A red butterfly with tattered, tarnished wings struggled inside the double-glazing. Nauseated, he studied the dusty glass, the dark poplars outside the window. He turned back to Olya, who was screwing up a little damp handkerchief. 'That's all. You can go. I've nothing else to say to you. What happens to you is up to the competent authorities. Report to the third floor, Room 27. They'll deal with you there.'

Olya stumbled out and climbed to the third floor, where, blinded by tears, she could scarcely find the door he had indicated. Before going in she took a quick look in her little

48

pocket mirror, fanned her swollen eyes with her hand and knocked.

Behind the desk a handsome man in his forties was talking on the telephone. He looked up at her, greeted her with a nod and, smiling, indicated the armchair. Olya sat down timidly on the edge of the seat. While continuing to give laconic replies, the man took a bottle of water out from under the desk and deftly opened it with one hand. He poured some into a glass and slid it gently across towards Olya, blinked and smiled at her again. 'He doesn't know why I'm here yet,' she thought, swallowing a little sparkling mouthful. 'When he discovers he'll yell at me and throw me out.'

The man put down the receiver, extracted a sheet of paper from a drawer and scanned it quickly. He studied his visitor and said: 'Good. Olga Ivanovna Demidova, if I'm not mistaken? Well, Olya, let's get to know one another.' And he introduced himself: 'Sergeï Nikolaievich.' Then he paused, sighed, rubbed his temples and went on, as if regretfully: 'You see, Olya, what took place is without any doubt unfortunate and, I fear, heavy with consequences for you. As a man, I can understand you: youth's the season made for joy, of course. You yearn for new sensations . . . Essenin, you remember, calls it: "the flood tide of feelings" – that's his phrase, isn't it? But that's the poet speaking. And you and I are living in the world of political and ideological realities. Today your Frenchman is throwing the javelin or doing the high jump. Tomorrow he's being trained for some kind of intelligence work and comes back here as a spy. Well, I'm not going to make a speech. You've already had enough of an earful. I'm just going to say one thing to you. We, for our part, will do everything possible to get you out of trouble. You understand, no one wants to cast a shadow over your father; and you yourself, we don't want to ruin your future. But for your part you must help us. I shall have to talk about this whole business to my superiors.

49

And so, to make sure that I don't give them a cock-and-bull story, we're going to put it all down in black and white. Right, here's some paper. As to the form of words, I'll help you.'

When Olya emerged from Room 27 an hour later, she felt as if, with a kick of her heels, she could have taken flight. How ridiculous he seemed to her now, that *Komsomol* official with his glistening pate!

She had just had fleeting contact with the mechanism of real power in the country. Filled with wonder, she found a way to spell out to herself, in naïve but accurate enough terms, all that had happened: 'The KGB can do anything.'

That evening, however, she was seized by an impression quite different from that of the morning. She recalled a sentence she had written in Room 27. Describing that first evening with Jean-Claude she had written: 'Finding myself in the bedroom of the French athlete, Berthet, Jean-Claude . . . I engaged in intimate relations with him.' It was that sentence that jarred. 'Intimate relations,' she thought. 'What an odd turn of phrase! And yet, basically, why odd? That's all it was. Certainly not love, in any event . . .'

She only saw Jean-Claude one more time and, as the polite man in Room 27 had advised, had spoken a few friendly words to him and slipped away.

On the day before the athletes left she came across him in the company of a friend. The two men passed quite close by without noticing her. The friend was patting Jean-Claude on the shoulder and he was smiling with a contented air. Olya heard Jean-Claude remarking somewhat languidly, drawing out the syllables: 'You know, I think I'm going ahead with that property in the Vendée. They simply hand the house over to you, with the keys: no problem.'

'Is Fabienne happy with that?' asked the other.

'Absolutely! She adores sailing!'

* * *

50

In the spring of 1982 no one in the country yet knew that it was going to be a quite extraordinary year. In November Brezhnev would die and Andropov would accede to the throne. The liberal intelligentsia, gathered in their kitchens, would begin to be tormented by the worst forebodings. Everyone knows he was once the head of the KGB. He's bound to crack down hard. Under Brezhnev you could still risk opening your mouth from time to time. Now there's going to be a reaction, that's for sure. They say he's already ordering police raids in the streets. You step out of your office for five minutes and the militia pounce on you. Let's hope it's not going to be another 1937 . . .

But History, as like as not, had had enough of the dreary monolithic solemnity of those long decades of socialism and decided to have a bit of fun. The man whose character the alarmed intellectuals identified as that of another 'Father of all the Peoples', or even another 'Iron Felix' Dzerzhinsky, turned out to be a mortally weary and sick monarch. He knew that the majority of the members of the Politburo ought to be put up against a wall and shot. He knew that the Minister of the Interior, with whom he chatted amiably on the telephone, was a criminal against the state. He knew how much each of his colleagues in the Politburo had in Western bank accounts. He even knew the names of the banks. He knew that a feudal system had long since been reinstated in Central Asia and that the right place for all those responsible was prison. He knew that in Afghanistan the American scenario in Vietnam was being replicated. He knew that in the villages in the whole of the North West, there was a shortage of bread. He knew that for a long time now the country had been run by a small family mafia who detested him personally, and who despised the people. He knew that if the rouble had been convertible half the country's rulers would have decamped to Miami or elsewhere long ago. He knew that the dissidents in prison or in exile did not know the hundredth part of what he knew and that the things they commented on were small beer. He knew so many things about this society that one day at the Party Plenum he let slip: 'We have no cognizance of the society in which we live.'

History had its little joke. The terror this man inspired in some and the hope he inspired in others both arose, as it were, from beyond the grave. He was dying of nephritis and in his moments of lucidity used to derive amusement from a story he had been told by the Kremlin doctor. It tickled him greatly. It happens during a meeting of the Politburo. They are all discussing who is to succeed Brezhnev. Suddenly the door is flung open and Andropov bursts in, accompanied by Aliev. Brandishing a revolver, Andropov shouts: 'Hands up!' All the old men raise their trembling hands. 'Lower the left hand!' commands Andropov. Turning to Aliev, he says: 'Make a note! A unanimous vote for Andropov!'

History delighted in making a mockery of those who thought they could determine its course with impunity. Andropov died. Chernenko followed him. With the indecent haste of a comic strip, all Brezhnev's entourage were dying off. They celebrated funeral rites to the tune of Chopin's funeral march on Red Square so often that the people of Moscow found themselves whistling the tune as if it were a current popular song.

But in the spring of 1982 no one could even imagine that History might get up to such tricks.

In March the head of the transport organization called Demidov into his office. 'You've got visitors, Ivan Dmitrevich. These comrades are going to make a film about you.' Two television journalists from Moscow were there, the scriptwriter and the director.

The film in question was to be devoted to the fortieth anniversary of the battle of Stalingrad. They had already shot the scenes of the Memorial Ceremony where, beneath the enormous concrete monuments, veterans from all four corners of the country wandered like ghosts from the past.

They had rediscovered documentary footage from the period, fragments of which they intended to use in the course of the film. They had already interviewed the generals and marshals who were still alive. What remained to be filmed was, in the eyes of the director, a very important episode. In this scene the principal role fell to Demidov. The director saw it like this: after the *dachas* in the outskirts of Moscow and the spacious Moscow apartments, where the retired marshals, buttoned up tight in their uniforms, command armies and juggle with brigades in their memory, there appear the twisting streets of Borissov and a lorry splashed with mud driving in at the entrance to a garage. A man gets down from the lorry, without turning towards the camera, wearing a battered cap and an old leather jacket. He crosses the yard littered with scrap iron, and makes his way over to the little office building. A somewhat metallic voice-over raps out the citation of the Hero of the Soviet Union: 'By the decree of the Supreme Soviet of the Union of Soviet Socialist Republics, for heroism and bravery displayed in battle . . .'

The lorry driver hands in some papers at the office, nods to a colleague, shakes hands with another and goes home.

In the course of this scene Demidov's voice, a simple, informal voice, talks about the battle of Stalingrad. The sequence of shots which follows is in the context of a home: the celebratory meal; a spread out copy of *Pravda* on a set of shelves; yellowing photographs of the post-war years on the wall.

But the high point of the film was elsewhere. From time to time the story of this modest hero 'who saved the world from the brown plague', as the commentary put it, breaks off. The Soviet foreign correspondent in one or other European capital appears on the screen, stopping passers-by and asking them:

'Tell me, what does the name of Stalingrad mean to you?' The passers-by hesitate, make inept replies and laughingly recall Stalin.

As for the correspondent in Paris, he had been filmed in melting snow, chilled to the bone, trying to make himself heard above the noise of the street: 'I'm standing just ten minutes' walk away from the square in Paris that bears the name of Stalingrad. But do the Parisians grasp the significance of this name, so foreign to French ears?' And he begins to question passers-by, who prove incapable of giving an answer.

When they showed this scene for the first time at the studio one of the bosses asked the director: 'So why couldn't he go to the square itself? What's all that about: "just ten minutes' walk away from"? It's like doing a report on Red Square from Gorky Park!'

'I already asked him that . . .' the director tried to excuse himself. 'According to him, there's not a Frenchman to be found in the square. Nothing but Blacks and Arabs. Yes, that's what he said. I give you my word. He said: "They'll all think it was shot in Africa and not in Paris at all." That's why he moved closer to the centre to find some Whites.'

'Unbelievable!' bayed an official in the darkened auditorium. And the showing continued. The camera focused on a huddled *clochard* and a row of gleaming shop windows. And then once more there appeared yellowing shots of documentary footage from the period: the grey steppe, tanks bobbing up and down, as if at sea, soldiers captured, still alive, on camera.

And Demidov appeared once more, no longer in his grease-stained jacket but in a suit, wearing all his decorations. He was in a classroom, seated behind a desk, that was decked out with a little vase containing three red carnations. In front of him schoolchildren were religiously drinking in his words.

The film ended with an apotheosis: the gigantic statue of the

Mother Country, holding a sword aloft, towered up into the blue sky. Then the Victory Parade taking place on Red Square in 1945. The soldiers throwing down German flags at the foot of the Lenin Mausoleum. Hitler's personal standard could be seen in the foreground as it fell. After that, against the exultant sound of music, Stalingrad-Volgograd, in all its splendour, arisen once more from the ruins, filmed from a helicopter.

And everything concluded with one final chord: Brezhnev appearing on the platform at the twenty-sixth Party Congress, talking about the Soviet Union's policies for peace.

By about the middle of April the film was ready. Demidov had patiently endured the excitement of the filming and, in answering questions, had even managed to include the story of the little wellspring in the wood.

'Well now, Ivan Dmitrevich,' the director said to him, when it was time to say goodbye. 'On Victory Day, 9 May, or perhaps the day before, you must sit down with all the family in front of the television.'

The film was called: *The Heroic City on the Volga*.

On the afternoon of 8 May, Ivan Dmitrevich was not working. He had been invited to the school for the traditional chat. He gave his usual talk and returned home with the three carnations in his hand.

Tatyana was still at work. He pottered about in the flat. Then he draped his best jacket, with its armour plating of medals, over the back of a chair, switched on the set and settled himself down on the divan. The film about Stalingrad was due to start at six.

The workshop foreman flourished the bottle and began pouring alcohol into the glasses: 'Very good, my friends, one last nip and we all go home . . .' They all drank, slipped what remained of the food into their bags and left. In the street the women workers wished one another a happy holiday and went back to their lodgings.

Tanya – no longer a girl, she was now always known as Tatyana Kuzminichna – consulted her watch. 'I've just enough time before the film to go to the shop and pick up the Veterans' parcel.' Like all those who had served in the war, she would receive this package in the section of the shop closed to ordinary mortals. People would watch the queue of Veterans there and quietly grumble.

This time it was a real holiday parcel: four hundred grams of ham, two chickens, a tin of sprats and a kilo of buckwheat flour. Tatyana Kuzminichna paid, loaded it all into her bag and started for the door. One of the Veterans called out to her.

'Hullo there, Kuzminichna, is it a good one, today's parcel?'

'Yes, not bad. But there's no butter.'

'There's butter to be had across the road today, at the Gastronom. But there's a queue a mile long!'

Tatyana went over to the Gastronom shop, saw a motley, winding queue, looked at the time. The film was due to start in fifteen minutes. 'Why not try to avoid queuing?' she thought. 'After all, it's my right.' She took her Veteran's pass out of her bag and began to push her way towards the till.

The tail end of the queue swarmed out into the street and inside the shop everything was dark with people. They pressed against one another, beating a path towards the counter. They shouted, they hurled insults at one another. The ones who had already made their purchases were weaving their way towards the exit, their eyes shining feverishly.

'How many packs per person?' the people at the back of the queue shouted from the street.

'Two each,' replied the people in the middle.

'Give me six,' whined a woman, close to the counter. 'I'll take my children's as well.'

'And where are they, your children?' enquired the exasperated sales assistant.

'Well, here she is, this little girl!' exclaimed the woman tugging at the hand of a frightened schoolgirl with a satchel.

'And where's the other one?' insisted the sales assistant.

'Out there in the street, in the push-chair.'

The woman, who had finally got her way, rushed towards the exit, clutching the six packs of butter to her chest.

A somewhat tipsy little bystander called out merrily: 'But they're not her kids! I know her. She doesn't have any kids. She's borrowed them from her sister! Ha ha ha!'

The queue gave a spasmodic shudder and moved a pace forwards. The manager appeared from the doorway to the storeroom, walked through the shop and called towards the end of the queue, which was getting longer. 'Don't push your luck at the back there. The butter's almost run out. Only three more cases. It's not worth your waiting. At all events, there won't be enough for everyone. You're wasting your time.'

But the people kept flocking up, asking who was the last and joining the queue. And each of them was thinking: 'Who knows? Maybe there'll still be enough for me!'

Tanya reached the till and, over the head of another woman, held out a crumpled three-rouble note and her Veteran's pass. She was not expecting such a unanimous explosion. The crowd seethed and bellowed with one voice. 'Don't let her go in front of the others!'

'Isn't that just typical! These Veterans! Let them buy their butter in their own shop!'

'They already give them parcels. And we've been waiting here with the children for three hours!'

'My son was killed in Afghanistan. But I don't give myself airs. I wait my turn like everyone else.'

'Don't give her anything! They have enough privileges as it is.'

Someone gave her a shove with their shoulder, the crowd

57

gave a slithery twitch and slowly edged her away from the till. Tatyana did not argue, gripped the money and the book in her injured hand and went back towards the exit to join the queue. The crowd was so dense that different queues were mingling together. Afraid of losing their places, people pressed against one another. Suddenly someone tugged at Tatyana's sleeve.

'Kuzminichna, come in front of me. Maybe we can get some of this butter.'

It was the old caretaker from their factory, Aunt Valya. Tatyana stood beside her and, so as to lull the vigilance of the people behind, they began chatting quietly together. After a moment Tatyana slipped into the throng without anyone noticing. Aunt Valya was halfway along.

'It's not too bad. This lot won't take more than an hour,' she remarked. 'We'll get there before they close. As long as there's still some butter left!'

Tatyana looked at her watch. It was six o'clock. 'It's a shame, I'm going to miss the film about Ivan,' she thought. 'But it's on again tomorrow morning.'

'That's odd, Tatyana's still not back,' thought Ivan. 'She must be traipsing round the shops. Never mind. She'll see it tomorrow.'

On the screen a marshal was already talking in a solemn bass voice and a restless reporter with prying eyes was asking him questions. This was followed by the jerky sequence of documentary footage from the period: the buildings of Stalingrad gently collapsing amid black clouds, as if in a state of weightlessness, beneath silent explosions.

When these shots were shown Ivan could not hold back his tears. 'I've become an old man,' he thought, biting his lip. His chin trembled slightly. From time to time he made silent comments to the soldiers running across the screen: 'Just look at that idiot running along without keeping his head down!

Get down, get down for heaven's sake, imbecile ... Pooh! And they call that an attack! They're rushing straight into the enemy machine gun fire without artillery support! By the look of it, there are so many people in Russia that soldiers don't matter!'

At length Ivan himself appeared on the screen. He froze, listening to every one of his own words, not recognizing himself. 'And then, after that battle,' he was saying, 'I went into ... there was this little wood there ... I look and what I see is a spring. The water's so pure! I lean over and see my own reflection ... It was very strange, you know. I'm looking at myself and I don't recognize myself ...' Here his story broke off and the voice-over, warm and penetrating, took up the tale: 'The native soil ... the soil of the Mother Country ... This was what gave strength to the weary soldier, this was the truly maternal care that nurtured his courage and bravery. It was from this inexhaustible wellspring that the Soviet fighter drew his revivifying joy, the sacred hatred of the enemy, the unshakeable faith in Victory ...'

The sales assistant, trying to be heard above the noise of the crowd, shouted in a strident voice: 'The butter's finished!' and, turning towards the cashier, added in even more ringing tones: 'Lyuda, don't make out any more tickets for butter.'

Tanya was handed two packs from the bottom of the third case. The last two went to Aunt Valya. They smiled at one another as they put them into their bags and began to elbow their way towards the exit.

The disappointed crowd froze for a moment, as if unable to believe all that time had been spent in vain, then shook itself and began to trickle slowly through the narrow door. Meanwhile there were people trying to squeeze in from outside who did not know the sale of butter was finished. At that moment a rumour began to circulate. Sausage had been delivered. The whole crowd flowed back towards the counter, forming into a queue once more. More people than ever piled in from the street.

The news reached the manager's ears. She emerged from the storeroom again and bellowed out in a mocking voice, as if she were speaking to children: 'What's all this then? You must be out of your minds. What's all this about sausage? There's not a scrap of sausage here. And anyway we're closing in half an hour.'

And now all anyone could think of doing was getting away. It was stiflingly hot in this compact mass of humanity. Tatyana was trying not to lose Aunt Valya, who was weaving her way very adroitly towards the door.

Everyone was infuriated. They took a malign pleasure in jostling one another, eager for an opportunity to exchange insults. Tatyana was already very close to the exit when she was swept away, as if by a whirlwind, and pinned up against a wall. Someone's shoulder – she was aware of a woman's blue raincoat – pressed hard into her breast. She tried to break free but did not succeed, so densely packed was the crowd. Her very powerlessness seemed to her ridiculous. She tried to transfer her bag to her other hand but just at that moment was surprised to feel she could no longer breathe. Suddenly there was a silence, as if deep under water, and now she could make out all too clearly the grey cloth of the coat barring her way. When, with the time lag of a distant explosion, the pain swept over her, she could not even utter a cry.

She was borne to the front of the building by a closely packed crowd . . . No one had noticed a thing. It was only on the steps that, as it dispersed, the crowd let her go. Tatyana collapsed gently. The butter and the Veteran's pass fell out of her bag. People stumbled against her body. Some moved away hastily, others bent over her. The merry little bystander roared with laughter. 'Well, what do you know? The little mother's taken a drop too many in advance of tomorrow's celebration!' Aunt Valya pushed aside the gaping onlookers, came up to her and called out in piercing tones: 'Help! Look! This woman's been taken ill! Quickly, someone call an ambulance!'

Ivan arrived at the hospital wearing the jacket of his best suit. He had hurried through the evening streets accompanied by the jangling of his decorations. He was not allowed into intensive care. He stared at the doctor who was making reassuring remarks to him but took nothing in. His Gold Star, which had turned back to front as he ran, looked like a child's toy.

The following morning, 9 May, the same doctor, reeking of tobacco, his face hollow from being on night duty, emerged and sat down in silence with Ivan on the wooden benches in the corridor. In some arcane corner of his mind, Ivan had already had time, not to consider what his life would be like without Tatyana, but to have a sharp and desperate presentiment of it. As this feeling welled up the echoing void alarmed him. He sat there without asking the doctor anything, following with an absent gaze the actions of an old cleaning woman as she wiped the dusty windows.

Finally the doctor gave a sigh and said softly: 'She should never have risked herself in our crowds. For her even wiping a window was dangerous.'

Olya arrived the next day. She was so beautiful it was almost unseemly. She herself felt uneasy with her tight skirt and the sound of her high heels in their now silent flat, amid the whispers of people dressed in black whom she hardly knew. One of the women gave her a black headscarf for the funeral. But even with this scarf her beauty was astonishing. She wept a great deal. What devastated her was not so much the grim, emaciated face of her mother, as the fragility of everything she had believed to be so natural and solid. Everything was crumbling before her eyes. From being a dashing hero, her father had turned into an old fellow with all the stuffing knocked out of him and red eyes. Now her parents' lives struck her as unbelievably drab. A wretched, starved childhood, the war, more starvation and then right up to old age – no, right up to death itself – that absurd furniture factory, and that lorry driver's cab, stinking of diesel oil. Olya looked around her in astonishment. The television her parents sat in front of each evening. The sofa bed where they slept. A photo on the bedside table: the two of them, still very young, before she was born, somewhere in the south, during the course of the only holiday trip of their lives. And just this photo, her father's sandals – horrible sandals, reminiscent of dog muzzles – just her mother's gesture, hiding her right hand, all this was enough to break her heart.

Ivan hardly saw anything of his daughter. It was only on the last night, when the weary relatives had left them, that he came face to face with Olya. They were sitting one each side of the coffin, completely exhausted by the ceaseless agitation of the women fussing about, by all the day's endless and meaningless whisperings. Ivan looked at his daughter and thought: 'She's a woman now. She's of an age to get married. It seems only yesterday that Tatyana was wrapping her in swaddling clothes. How time flies! Day nursery, school and now Moscow, the Institute . . . She needs to find a good lad, one who doesn't drink . . . A soldier . . . Although that lot hit the bottle these days like nobody's business! I must speak to her. Now that we're burying her mother . . .'

It was only at the station, when they were waiting for the Moscow train, that Ivan said to her: 'You must work hard, Olya. Just . . .' Olya laughed sweetly.

'But Dad, I've only got a few more weeks of classes. I'm just about to do my final exams.'

'Oh, really?' said Ivan, amazed and embarrassed. 'So where will you go after that?'

'Wherever my Country calls me to serve,' joked Olya.

She kissed Ivan and boarded the train. She waved to her father through the window for a long time, as he stood motionless in his tired dark suit on the platform flooded with sunlight.

Olya already knew where her Country would call her to serve ... Some of the students in her year expected to make a painless transfer from lecture room benches to well-upholstered chairs lined up for them by their relatives in high places. Others resignedly prepared themselves for the drudgery of technical translations in a dusty office. Yet others dreamed of immersing themselves as soon as possible in the whirl of Intourist, anticipating with delight the cavalcade of European faces passing by too rapidly to grow wearisome, thrilled, in advance, to think of all those little presents and the mirage of Western life.

For Olya it was quite different. Sergeï Nikolaievich of Room 27 had long since been replaced by his equally impressive colleague, Vitaly Ivanovich. It was when she met him in April that Olya learned where her Country would call her to serve.

They were in a hotel room, which was where their meetings often took place. Vitaly Ivanovich was smiling mysteriously and rubbing his hands, like a man who has a pleasant surprise up his sleeve. They were talking about their current business, the foreigner whom Olya was taking care of at the time. Then, as if he had suddenly remembered something, Vitaly Ivanovich exclaimed: 'Listen, Olya! You'll soon be finished at your Institute. Then it'll be time for appointments. Have you already had preliminary appointments? ... So, what sector have they assigned you to? ... Well, obviously! Technical translation relating to patents in a factory. It's not the greatest fun in the world. What are you planning to do? ... But no, listen. You shouldn't be such a pessimist. There'll be time enough for you to bury yourself in all that dust. I've talked about this with my superiors. Your services are greatly appreciated. That's why it's been decided to recommend you – not officially, you understand – for work as an interpreter at the International Trade Centre . . . Hold on, don't get carried away. Save your thanks for later. I don't think there's any need for me to explain to you that at the Centre there are hundreds and thousands of foreigners. And so, our specific work, intelligence and counter-espionage, as they call it in the detective stories, takes precedence . . .'

Olya went out feeling slightly dizzy. She walked along the grey April streets where the red flags for the May celebrations were already unfurled. On the front of a big department store workmen were fixing up an enormous banner with portraits of Marx, Engels and Lenin. The red canvas was not yet stretched taut and the April wind was making it belly out in little ripples. At one moment the prophets of Marxism were gazing out over the roofs of Moscow towards the radiant future, and the next they were winking ambiguously at the passers-by.

Olya walked the full length of the Kalininsky Prospekt in a state of blissful giddiness. Now even its hideous concrete skyscrapers seemed to her graceful. She descended towards the Moskva River and climbed up onto the bridge. Everything in this part of Moscow is on a gigantic and inhuman scale. The seven hundred foot pyramid of Moscow State University can be seen silhouetted against the skyline. On the other side of the river, with the same exuberance of Stalinist gothic, the building of the Ukraïna Hotel thrusts upwards into the sky. Behind it glitters the COMECON skyscraper's open book. On the opposite bank, facing the Ukraïna, stands a collection of grey-green buildings with orange windows. It is precisely there that the International Trade Centre is located.

On the bridge a strong and supple wind was blowing. Olya felt as if her short hair were billowing out like a long silken train. She had never felt so young and free. All over again she was thinking, with a smile of admiration; the KGB can do anything!

During those two years that had followed the Olympic Games Olya had come to understand what Vitaly Ivanovich had referred to as the very 'specific' nature of that work. Now she knew what interested him and his colleagues. And she knew how to extract this skilfully from a foreigner. How ridiculous that ruse of Jean-Claude's seemed to her now, suddenly needing a translation! She used it quite often herself these days, in order to establish contact with 'interesting' foreigners. But she had a great many other tricks, too. The names of her foreign acquaintances made up a continual procession: each one might last for a week, or a month, or a year. There was a certain Richard, an Alain ... a John, a Jonathan, a Steven ... Indeed, there were even two Jonathans, one English, one American. Their voices jostled one another in her memory in a confused chorus. Snatches of their confidences rose to the surface. One of them bore the title of 'Honourable' and was very proud of it. Another was an enthusiastic mountaineer and went rock-climbing in New Zealand. Another used to assert that everywhere you go in the USSR you run into people from the KGB. All of this and much more besides was passed on in the reports Olya diligently submitted to Vitaly Ivanovich. And sometimes details no one had any use for resurfaced, even though the people to whom they belonged had become confused in her memory: a shoulder covered in freckles, the glow from a face that resembled a pale mask in the heavy darkness of the bedroom ...

Sometimes, waking in the small hours, the favourite time for suicides, she was almost physically aware of the echoing void entering her eyes. She would prop herself up on one elbow, contemplating with alarmed amazement a head, a somewhat prominent ear, a half-open mouth from which a quiet little whistling sound emerged. Then her glance would turn towards the pile of crumpled clothes on the chair, and meet the languid eye of a saxophone player with dark slicked back hair, smiling at her from the wall. 'Gianni Caporale', she read on the poster. Sometimes in this darkness her stare would encounter that of a voluptuous half-naked beauty, or that of Lenin, stuck above the bed by a facetious Westerner. 'Gianni Caporale,' she read silently and took fright at her own internal voice. 'What am I doing here?' The question echoed in her head. And each time this 'I' reminded her of their flat in Borissov, the particular smell and light of their rooms. Also of a winter's day with sparkling sunshine, and a gleaming slope, with skiers and children on toboggans racing down it. That day – it must have been a Sunday – her parents were out for a walk with her. When she became tired of her toboggan Ivan thought it would be fun to invite her mother to have a ride. And, elated by the sun and the sharp, icy air, she laughingly agreed. They plunged down, so huge and so comic on the little toboggan! At the bottom they had overturned and then climbed back up the slope hand in hand, reappearing at the summit with rosy cheeks and shining eyes.

Olya looked again at the person sleeping beside her. She called him silently by his name, remembering what she knew of him in an effort to bring him to life, to bring him closer to herself, but it all remained empty of meaning.

'I'm nothing but a whore,' she said to herself. But she knew very well this was not true. 'What do I get out of all this? Tights from the Beriozka shop. That filthy make-up you can buy from any black-market dealer . . . I should really stop this at once. Vitaly Ivanovich? Well, so what? I could go and see him and tell him straight out: "I've had enough of this. It's finished. I'm getting married." They wouldn't put me in prison for that . . .'

These nocturnal reflections calmed her somewhat. 'I'm complicating my life,' she thought. 'I'm filling my head with all this nonsense. As Mayakovsky said: "What is good? What is evil?" And after all, where's the harm in it? The girls at the Institute hang about in restaurants for months before landing themselves some grubby little Yugoslav. While here there's something to suit all tastes ... Take Milka Vorontsova, a beautiful girl with real class, a princess. She found herself a husband, an African, without turning a hair!'

Olya remembered that after the three days of wedding celebrations Milka had gone back to the Institute. In the intervals between classes her fellow students had clustered round her and, with many a mischievous wink, had begun to ask her questions about the initial delights of conjugal life. Without any embarrassment and indeed welcoming this curiosity, Milka instructed them thus: 'Listen to me, you future "heroic mothers". The golden rule with an African husband is never to dream of him at night.'

'Why not?' the voices asked in amazement.

'Because he's so ugly that if you see him in your dreams there's a good chance you'll never wake again!'

There were peals of laughter. When the tinny sound of the bell rang out the students hastily stubbed out their cigarettes and made their way back to the lecture room. Olya asked Milka, 'Listen, Milka, are you really going to become African and live in Tamba-Dabatu?' Milka looked at her with her clear blue eyes and said softly: 'Olyechka, any town in the world can be a staging post to somewhere else!'

Outside the window the day was beginning to break. The head on the pillow murmured something in French and turned over onto the other cheek. Olya stretched out as well, unfolding her weary elbow with relief. The suicides' hour receded, as did the dark shadow of night.

In her new life at the Centre Olya's first 'client' was the representative of an English electronics firm. She made contact with him by telephone and introduced herself, saying that she was going to be his interpreter. The voice on the telephone was calm, self-confident, even a little authoritarian. She imagined a face in the manner of James Bond, with greying temples and a suit as dark as if it had been carved out of a block of granite glinting with mica. 'He's an old hand,' Sergeï Alexeievich, the KGB officer who worked with her at the Centre, had remarked of this Englishman. 'He knows the USSR very well and speaks Russian. But he pretends not to . . .'

But the imposing tones of the voice on the telephone had misled her. They were simply the tones formed by his profession. When a podgy, bald man clad in a checked jacket detached himself from the wall and came towards her in the lobby with a somewhat embarrassed smile, Olya was dumbfounded. He was already nodding his head and holding out his hand as he introduced himself while she continued to stare at him. At that very moment a metal cockerel began leaping up and down on its perch in the middle of the lobby, announcing twelve noon by flapping its wings. 'What an odd representative,' thought Olya in the lift.

When taking his shower that morning, the Englishman had lost a contact lens. Feeling around in the shower tray for it, he had lost the other one. Once dressed, he had extracted his glasses case from the bottom of his suitcase, taken his glasses out nervously and dropped them on a marble ash-tray. 'How can one present oneself in such a state?' thought Olya in amazement. He cast rather embarrassed glances at her: the right-hand lens of his spectacles was missing and his eye peered through the empty circle in a blurred and timid manner.

'I can understand almost everything in Russian,' he had said in the lift, 'but I'm out of practice and I speak it very badly.' He would say: 'I telephone to you,' and, something that particularly amused Olya, 'would you like to close me the door?' He was staying at the Intourist Hotel. On the third evening they had dinner together at the restaurant and she stayed with him.

And once more she experienced that hollow wakefulness early in the morning at the suicides' hour. But also, on this occasion, a calm, desperate serenity. She realized that what tormented her was not futile remorse but the inevitable disappointment of an absurd hope. It was something she had already experienced when she was at the Institute and was now encountering again at the Centre.

She used to meet a new 'subject' and, in spite of herself, without being conscious of it, would begin looking forward to some miraculous change, a completely new life that would be quite unlike the old one.

But nothing would change. Sometimes she would go with her acquaintances to the airport. Sluggishly, as if in an underwater kingdom, the announcements at Sheremetevo would make themselves heard. And already on the far side of customs, her 'subject' would be waving goodbye to her and disappearing amid the colourful crowd of passengers. She would walk away slowly towards the bus stop.

Nothing did change.

And now, waking up beside this Englishman, fast asleep, with his face in the pillow, she finally understood that she should expect nothing. That all this was futile. Futile, this hoping for something. And sometimes there was this feeling of pity for the 'subject', a sentient human being, after all. And a vague sense of shame.

She had to press on, knowing her place in the long, invisible chain that disappeared into the labyrinth of political games and technological theft, and ended up somewhere in the capitals of Europe and the Americas. It was not her business to think about all these machinations. Her business was to assess her 'subject' in a swift exchange of words and looks and, within a given time, to act out all the scenes of the stipulated love drama. Her business, when she encountered a representative like this in a checked jacket, was to make him forget that his damp reddish hair barely covered his bald head and that his right eye was peering out hazily and timidly, and that, in unbuttoning his crumpled shirt beneath his belt, he had laid bare his white belly and tried to cover it up and then, having caught her look, been horribly embarrassed.

In this first role at the Centre Olya played her part so well that the Englishman did not dare to give her money. When she went with him to Sheremetevo he awkwardly presented her with an extremely costly perfume with the price ticket from Beriozka scratched off.

She remembered him well, this first client, and could recall some features of the next two. As for the rest, they soon became mixed up in her memory.

With her colleague, Svetka Samoïlova, Olya had rented two rooms, not far from the Belayevo area. Svetka had already been working at the Centre for two years. She was exceptionally greedy for Western currency and lingerie but at the same time extravagant and generous to a fault, in the Russian manner.

She had a beautiful and opulent physique. If she had not succeeded in holding herself in check in Moscow, she would long since have turned into an Arkhangelsk matron, a human mountain, robust and warm-blooded. In Moscow, on the other hand, and especially at the Centre, she had been obliged to go against all the dictates of her nature. She was constantly on a diet, forced herself to drink tea without sugar and, in particular, exercised with a hula-hoop at every free moment. The fashion for this had passed years ago but it was not a question of fashion. Svetka had pierced a hole in her hula-hoop, slipped half a pound of lead into it and sealed it up again with adhesive tape. It had become a weighty contraption. She spun it in the kitchen when stirring clear semolina, on the telephone, in her room in front of the television.

They often spent their free evenings in Svetka's room, chatting or watching the innumerable episodes of some adventure film.

Olya occasionally went in there when Svetka was away, sometimes to borrow the iron, sometimes to leave on the bed a letter bearing the crude postmark of a village to the north of Arkhangelsk.

At such moments Svetka's room appeared to her in a completely different, unaccustomed light. Her gaze took in the narrow work table, the coffee table piled high with old Western magazines, the arabesques on a thick carpet. And she no longer recognized any of it.

There was the chipped bottom half of a Russian doll, bristling with pencils, a glass saucer glittering with bracelets and earrings and, open on a pile of magazines, a little book printed on grey paper, *Autumn Cicadas*.

Olya bent over it. A three-line stanza had a mark in the margin against it made with a fingernail:

> Life is a field in which, as darkness falls,
> Close to the footpath, there amid the corn,
> A tiger watches, eagerly alert.

Olya studied everything around her with uneasy curiosity. It was as if the things all took pleasure in the places where they had been put. Among these objects Olya had a presentiment of hope for some alleviation, the possibility of becoming reconciled to all that she lived through each day. To her amazement she seemed to be making a strange excursion into this anticipated future, without knowing if this was encouraging or a cause for despair.

She found herself picking up the heavy hula-hoop behind the dressing-table and, for amusement, tried to spin it round, imitating Svetka's gyrations. She recalled her friend's joking observation: 'Do you remember who coined this gem? Was it Breton? Aragon? "I saw a woman-waisted wasp pass by."'

'Absolutely. One with hips like an Arkhangelsk milk-delivery woman,' Olya had teased her.

'You may laugh! But when you're older you'll understand that real men always appreciate the poetry of contrast!'

And Svetka had made her contraption spin so fast that it hissed with the menacing fury of an aggressive insect . . .

On Svetka's dressing-table, among the bottles and the jars of make-up, there was a piece of paper covered in figures. Every week she measured herself. Sometimes Olya added a few wild noughts to the figures, or altered centimetres to cubic centimetres. Which sent them both into fits of laughter.

Amid the disorder of all the objects accumulated on Svetka's dressing-table stood two photos in identical frames. The first showed an elegant sunburnt officer with one eyebrow slightly raised. At the bottom of the photo the white lettering stood out clearly: 'To my dear Svetka, Volodya. Tashkent 1983.' In the other one a man and a woman, not yet old, pressed awkwardly shoulder to shoulder, were looking straight in front of them, without smiling. Their peasant faces were so simple and so open – almost unfashionable in this simplicity – that Olya always felt embarrassed by their silent gaze . . .

'It's curious,' she thought. 'What if Svetka's foreign clients were ever to see this hula-hoop, this photo, this "Tashkent 1983"? And that, too: "A tiger watches, eagerly alert"?'

Nevertheless from time to time Svetka's diet was put on hold. Noisily, and bringing the smell of snow with them, the guests would start to pile in, the table would be covered with food and wine. There was pale pink meat from the Beriozka shops, caviar and fillet of smoked sturgeon brought in from some ministry's private supply. Svetka pounced on the pastries, and cut herself a slice from a tart with baroque decorations, exclaiming with reckless bravado: 'What the hell! You only live once!'

The guests thronging around this food were colleagues from the Centre, people in business and men from the KGB who saw to the alcohol. On mornings after feasts like this they got up late. They went to the kitchen, brewed up very strong tea and spent a long time drinking it. Sometimes, unable to restrain herself, Svetka opened the refrigerator and took out some wine: 'To hell with them, all these pathetic representatives! What kind of a life is this? We can't even drink to get rid of a hangover . . .' And on this pretext they took out the rest of the cake, and the remains of the elegant tart, whose decorations were now in ruins . . .

During these vacant Sundays, Hungarian Ninka, a prostitute from the Centre, often came to see them. She was called that because her father had been a Hungarian member of the Komintern and it was claimed that he was related to Bela Kun. He had been in prison under Khrushchev and after his release had had time, a year before his death, to marry and have a child, and this was Ninka.

She passed on all the gossip from her world: the caretaker was becoming a real bastard! To let you into the Centre he now took fifteen roubles instead of ten! Broad-hipped Lyudka had managed to get herself married to her Spaniard . . . It was rumoured they were going to close the Beriozka shops . . .

These winter days passed slowly. Outside the windows occasional sleepy flakes fell from a dull sky. Under the window they could hear people from the flats beating their carpets on the snow. Children shouted on the frozen slide.

Sometimes, by way of a joke, Ninka and Svetka would start arguing: 'You've got it made,' the Hungarian would say. 'You sit there in the warm. Your salary arrives regularly. They bring you a client on a silver salver: "Here you are, Madam. Be so kind as to bid him welcome and look after him." Whereas we catch our death, just like those poor wretched whores at railway stations. The law get their three roubles from us. And our own mates, the damned bitches, are forever shopping us to cut out the competition . . .'

'You're breaking my heart! We've heard all that before . . .

The poor little orphan from Kazan . . .' Svetka cut in. 'I expect you'd like an extra milk allowance for dangerous work as well, wouldn't you? You're all millionaires, you lot. You talk about a salary . . . But that hardly keeps us in toilet paper. And you charge a hundred dollars for ten minutes. You said it yourself, you know, that one – what's her name, now? The one with big bosoms. She sleeps on a mattress stuffed with hundred-rouble notes.'

'A mattress?' gasped Olya.

'Yes,' Ninka took up the tale. 'She was scared to deposit her money in the savings bank. You see in theory she was working as a cleaner at the children's nursery; and she was worth maybe half a million . . . But where to hide it? So she began stuffing notes into the mattress. Her dream was to work like a horse till the age of thirty, then find a bloke, start a family and have a cushy life. But of course it was her bloke who did the dirty on her. As well as her foreigners, she had this Vladik, a Russian, all to herself, for a bit of romance . . . One night he can't stop fidgeting, something's getting to him, poking him in the ribs, crackling under him . . . And in the morning he has a brainwave! He waits for Sonka – Sophie, we call her – to go out and he undoes the stitching. And there, for God's sake, beneath a layer of foam, are hundred-rouble notes and wads of foreign currency – packed so tight you couldn't count them! But he was clever, the pig. No question of taking it all. Sonka's friends would have moved heaven and earth to hunt him down. He started taking it out a little bit at a time. And that's how he lived. She was earning it: he was burning it.'

'Men! They're all vampires!' sighed Svetka.

'So what happened in the end?' Olya wanted to know.

'It finished the way it was bound to, of course! Using her money, he picked up a girl and flew off to the Crimea with her for the weekend. He passed himself off as a diplomat. And why not? He was flashing wads of those mattress-stuffing dollars . . . Why shouldn't it be true? When Sonka found out at first she wanted to strangle him on that damned mattress that very night. But then she went all soft and forgave him everything!'

The grey winter's day sank gently into a silent and peaceful evening. And they were still chatting in the kitchen. Outside it began to freeze and voices sounded clearer and more resonant.

Hungarian Ninka was telling stories about her summer trips to Sochi, her quarrels with the local girls and how one day some completely drunken Finns had thrown her out into the corridor stark naked.

'And their lady wives, by the way, developed a taste for coming to stay here. They come to Leningrad for the weekend as tourists and then, instead of visiting the cruiser Aurora, they pick up clients by the shovelful. It was a girlfriend of mine who told me: they take all their trade. The militia leaves them alone. And that reminds me, she told me a good story. Four prostitutes meet: a Frenchwoman, an Englishwoman, a German and a Russian. They start arguing about which of the four is best at picking up men. They're all lined up on the corner of Gorky Street and Marx Avenue, near the Hotel National . . .'

At that moment a car started hooting noisily outside in the street. Ninka jumped up and ran to the window.

'Oh my goodness. My little friend's arrived. Right. I'm off.'

She finished the story in the hallway as she slipped into her fur coat and put on some lipstick.

'Hey, are you going to walk about barefoot all winter?' Svetka exclaimed in astonishment looking at her delicate ankle boots. 'Take care or your toes will freeze and then no more dollars to fill your mattress! And then what will you sleep on with your little friend?'

Adjusting her fox-fur hat in the mirror, Ninka answered

carelessly: 'Oh, you big softies! You princesses with your peas! You sit there in your offices next to your radiators. It's easy for you. You get driven all the way to the bedside in an official car. But we're out there on our feet in all weathers, like the sentries at the Mausoleum. Never mind ankle boots! Let me sell you my patent formula. When they kick you out of the Centre, you'll need it!'

'So what's this patent formula?' chorused Olya and Svetka in amazement.

'The patent formula. You buy a pepper poultice from the chemist, you cut it to the size of the sole of your foot and, hey presto, you stick it to your foot. It works like a mustard plaster but it lasts longer and it doesn't burn so much. It's thirty degrees below outside but you can go out in elegant shoes. You feel as warm inside as if you'd had a good nip of vodka. That's how it is, my dainty ducks. It's different from lolling about at the Kontik Hotel sipping cocktails.'

Under the window the car kept on hooting. 'All right, I'm coming,' grumbled Ninka. 'He can't stand being kept waiting, that one. Ankle boots from abroad. I've put them on specially for him. Maybe he'll marry me, the fallen woman . . .'

They chuckled heartily as they kissed and Ninka raced down the stairs, her heels clattering.

Outside the evening was turning blue. Olya washed up. Svetka sat slowly drinking what was left of the flat champagne and scrabbled about in the cake box for the little nuts that had fallen off.

'It's the last glass,' she excused herself. 'Tomorrow I'm starting a new life. Help! That parfumier's coming from Paris tomorrow and I have to get up at half past five . . .'

In the course of these evenings together Olya longed to talk openly to Svetka, to confide in her. To ask her, 'What about you, Svetka? Do you like this life? Aren't you ever scared? Scared of your youth passing away . . . And this whole routine . . . From the first meeting when everything

76

is official, the black shoes, the severe suit, the professional woman, Soviet style . . . until we get to the bed with Intourist sheets. Just the smell of them makes me want to throw up. Doesn't it scare you when you get one of these old fellows, you know, just on the brink of retirement, with a weedy body and scrawny armpits that already smell of the grave? The time it takes to get him warmed up, you're sweating like a masseuse or a nurse in intensive care. For the past ten years he's only been cheating on his wife with porn magazines, and now he's hungry for exotic Moscow nights, luscious Russian kisses . . . Doesn't all that make you want to throw up, Svetka? And yet with the young ones, it's even worse. At least the old ones don't take themselves too seriously. And they pay well. But these bastards think they're giving us a thrill with their biceps that stink of deodorant. And they're so mean with it! They won't part with half a cent. You'll never believe this. One day I was watching an Italian packing his bags. There was half a tin of meat paste left over from our breakfast. Well, he wrapped it in plastic and slipped it into his case. I said to him: "I'd get rid of that! It'll go off in the plane!" But that cut no ice with him. He laughed. "I'll have it for dinner tonight in Rome . . ." You go on waiting. You go on waiting, like an idiot. It's the same with you, Svetka, you're waiting too, only you won't admit it. And you go on spinning your hula-hoop like a robot . . .'

But Olya did not dare to say this to her so baldly. That evening she skated round it, making a joke of it. But Svetka understood at once what she was driving at.

'Olyechka, that's the semi-Muscovite coming out in you. Ninka was right: all on a silver salver! Moscow? Do me a favour! The Institute? Help yourself! The International Trade Centre? Come right in! You should have lived in the village of Tiomny Bor like me, up near Arkhangelsk, then you wouldn't be wallowing in this morass of existentialism. An eight-mile walk to school each day and it was so cold that when you spat it froze in the air and made a noise as it landed. When you started taking in the washing off the line it snapped in half. You take it into the house, you look at it and hey presto the shirt's lost its sleeves. And the people! Total savages! You can't imagine. Everyone's drunk. We had a neighbour. He and his wife were completely drunk every day. And a child every year. They had nine in all. All a bit cracked, of course. Thanks to the vodka, the parents had become complete zombies. A new child arrives and they give it the first name that comes into their heads. Afterwards they find they've got two Sergeïs and two Lyudkas ... And you talk about being scared? Now this is scary. Nothing in the shops but tinned mackerel in tomato sauce and weevily millet. That's all there is! And vodka, of course. The whole village goes to bed dead drunk and meanwhile the wolves snatch the dogs from their kennels. You talk about "our youth passing away". Well, where doesn't it pass away? A weedy body ... Well, hark at her! ... A smell of the grave ... You do talk a lot of rubbish, especially at bedtime. Now, just suppose you were married to a little Muscovite executive on a hundred and fifty roubles a month, do you think that'd be more fun? He'd never stop reminding you about his Moscow residence permit and his paltry square metres of living space. And where would you work? At the factory? Translating patents for a hundred and thirty roubles? At the end of a week you'd have such existential angst, you'd go and work as a cleaner at the Centre. You need to simmer down. No one's keeping you here. The KGB? Oh yes, you bet, they need you! They have only to whistle and people will come running from all over the Soviet Union to get their hands on your nice little job. They'll find more exciting girls than you to do it! You'd better believe it. You're too spoilt, that's your trouble. Look at Hungarian Ninka. No father or mother from the age of seven: brought up in an institution. And that's where one of the teachers assaulted her when she was fourteen, she told me. He took her into the showers and you can guess what happened next. In her place another woman would have become a drunkard and a wreck long ago, but she's as tough as old boots . . . She's treating herself to a co-operative flat in Yassenievo, buying herself a Volga, the latest model. She'll get married and everything'll be fine. She has about three hundred thousand roubles in different savings banks. While you're moaning about your pointless existence and the futility of waiting, she sticks mustard plasters to her feet and off she goes, all flags flying! So what about my Volodya, you say? But what difference does it make to him? Foreigners are work, not a love affair. And apart from them there's no other man in my life, you know that. Volodya has his military service. I can't go running after him to Afghanistan. And over there, by the way, you get promoted fast. In no time at all he'll have his colonel's three stars. Then we'll get married. And there'll be no more talk of foreigners. I'll ask for an office job at the Centre. Even now he's like a pig in clover. When he comes home on leave I stuff him with caviar and he gets to drink wine you won't find in most ministers' houses. And furthermore I'm a woman who gives him first-class service. So it'd be a great mistake for him to complain. Right, Olya. We've talked enough. Let's go and watch the news on television. It's odd . . . There's been no sign of Andropov for a long time. They say he's very ill. Oh look, you've done all the washing-up. You are sweet!'

Then, half stretched out on the divan, glancing absent-mindedly at the screen from time to time, she went on in a dreamy voice: 'You know, I sometimes get a bit of it myself too . . . The feeling that I've had enough. It all wells up inside me. You're in bed with this wretched capitalist and every time he breathes out he blows right in your ear . . . What misery! You tell yourself: "I was a schoolgirl in a white smock, I was waiting for Prince Charming in a star-spangled cloak . . ." Oh, and talking of princes, how's your prince from the World Youth Organisations Committee? You realize what a fiancé

I've introduced you to! And there you are, always complaining . . . A gift from the gods, a fiancé like that! Parents at COMECON, a four-roomed flat on Kutuzovsky Prospekt! You need to hold onto him tight. Don't let him fly away. You won't find yourself another one like that. A future diplomat!'

The weather forecast came on.

'Oh lordy!' groaned Svetka. 'Down to minus twenty-five. Right, tomorrow I'm going to buy some mustard plasters.'

'Everything's fine,' thought Olya. 'I did well to talk to Svetka. She's right, I think too much. Too much food spoils my appetite . . .'

She had got to know this prince from the World Youth Organisations Committee, Alexeï Babov, during the autumn. Svetka had invited him to their noisy parties. Since then Olya often used to meet him and sometimes he spent the night at her flat. Occasionally she visited him at his home. In his room there was a violin in its case on top of the wardrobe.

'Do you play?' she asked him one day.

'No, it was a youthful whim,' he remarked carelessly.

He tried to seem older than he was. His parents had rushed him into a career and this rapid ascent did not match his age. He dressed stylishly, teaming imported clothes with one another, as if in a mosaic: he sought out everything, down to his cufflinks. He had black hair, blue eyes and extremely soft skin on his cheeks. In their lovemaking Olya was at first surprised by the methodical nature and complexity of the positions he dreamed up. It was erotic acrobatics. One day, when looking through his library she found a book on the very top shelf, between a volume of international law and *Youth Organizations in France*: it was in French: *Le Savoir-faire Amoureux*. It went through the most improbable couplings with a succession of diagrams, like wrestling techniques. The door banged, Alexeï was returning. Olya quickly put the book back and jumped down off the chair . . .

* * *

Yes, truly, everything was going well. A lively job, a constant stream of faces and names, the upheavals that were a prelude to the new year. It was agreeable to give pleasure, to see this in the way well-groomed, self-confident men eyed her. Agreeable to be aware of her young, firm body, to picture her own face, her eyes, amid all this human activity in the capital. And to feel herself to be adult, independent and even a little aggressive.

Olya was unaware that, seen in profile and against the light, the glow of her face appeared almost transparent and juvenile in its delicacy, evocative of her mother's face at the same age. But that was something only her father saw. And even when he saw it his perception was filtered through such bitterness about the past that, in spite of himself, he would shake his head, as if to banish the fragile resemblance.

Three

'"No further retreat is possible," he says. "Behind us lies Moscow." And also behind us, for God's sake, was that line of machine guns! Ha ha ha! And now Gorbachev's going to screw the lot of them. You've read what it says about Brezhnev in *Izvestia*! "Stagnation," it says. "The mafia . . ." In the old days they talked about "developed socialism". Now that's what I'd call an about-turn! And on Stalin, too. Did you read it, Vanya? Krushchev's *Memoirs* . . . Nikita writes that when the war came Stalin was so scared he did it in his pants. He barricaded himself in his *dacha* and wouldn't let anyone in. He thought his number was up. They told us such fibs: "He organized the struggle . . . He drew up the strategy for victory . . ." Some bloody generalissimo!'

Ivan nodded his head gently, making the connection with some difficulty between the voice and the pale patch of a face hovering amid the pearly clouds of tobacco smoke. Waiters with the build of gorillas and the faces of bouncers threaded their way between the tables. Their fingers fanned out, carrying bunches of beer tankards.

By now Ivan was understanding almost nothing of what his neighbour was saying to him – the one who had served in Signals during the war. All he heard was: 'Stalin . . . Stalin . . .' And in a confused fashion this brought back an image from the past: the frozen expanse of Red Square, on 7 November 1941, the anniversary of the Revolution, the endless tide of soldiers chilled to the bone and finally himself amid these frozen ranks. The Mausoleum came into view, nearer and nearer. And already a whispering among the soldiers, like the murmuring of waves, runs through the ranks: 'Stalin . . . Stalin . . .' Suddenly he catches sight of him on the platform by the Mausoleum, amid clouds of frozen breath. Stalin! Calm, motionless, unshakeable. At the sight of him something almost animal thrills in each one of them. Each one of them believes Stalin is looking deeply into his eyes.

'Following this parade, the soldiers went straight to the front,' the confident voice of the commentator on the contemporary film footage would explain after the war. 'And each of them carried in his heart the unforgettable words of the Supreme Commander of the armies: "Our cause is just! Victory will be ours!"'

And they were marching, still marching, regiment upon regiment; with their eyes out on stalks, and reflected in them the crenellated walls of the Kremlin, the Mausoleum swathed in hoar-frost, looking as if it were made of white suede, and a man of average height, whose moustache was covered in silvery droplets . . .

A colossus appeared beside their table, a white napkin over his arm, gave the three drunken veterans a blasé look and sang out: 'All right, grandads, shall I fill them up or do you want to pay?'

'Go ahead, young man. We'll have one more for the road,' Ivan's neighbour bellowed. 'You see, we've just met up. We're almost all from the same regiment. We were on the same front in the war. But I was in Signals, Vanya was a gunner and Nikolaï . . .'

Amid hiccups he started relating his war experiences with sweeping gestures across the table. The waiter picked up the empty glasses and walked away, yawning, to get their beer.

What Ivan pictured now was not Red Square but a courtyard covered in mud, petrified by the cold, and the dry snow, surrounded by huts or barracks. They have penned the soldiers in there and kept them out in the icy wind for several hours. They have also brought in uncouth lads from the countryside on big farm carts, clad in wadded jackets, dishevelled *shapkas* and down-at-heel felt boots. No one knows what is going to happen next – if they will be sent straight to the front line or left there and fed, or stuck in the barracks to sleep on bunks. And the blue of the low winter sky slowly hardens. Dusk descends. It snows and still they are standing there, sunk in a drowsy, silent numbness. And suddenly, somewhere near the farm carts, the strident cry of a *garmoshka*, a little concertina, blares forth. One of the country lads is playing it, bare headed, with a mane of golden curls, not yet shorn, and a worn, unbuttoned sheepskin jacket . . . He is playing 'Yablochko' – little apple – a sailors' song; he plays with desperate passion, tugging furiously on his *garmoshka*. His unseeing gaze is lost in the distance, somewhere above the heads. In the midst of the soldiers who surround him a sailor dances with the same reckless passion, stamping his heels fiercely on the frozen earth. He is of middling height, stocky, with a craggy face. Sailor's jersey, black reefer jacket. He dances violently, baring his teeth in a wild fixed grin and he, too, stares at the grey horizon in blind ecstasy. The accordionist plays faster and faster, biting his lips and shaking his head in frenzy. The sailor stamps harder and harder upon the ground. Spellbound, the soldiers watch his face distorted with blissful agony. They no longer know where they are, they are no longer thinking about food, or sleep, or the front. The officer, who has come over to put an end to this merriment with one ear-splitting yell, stops and watches in silence. The sailor's boots are as heavy as if they were made of cast-iron. They are laced up with lengths of telephone wire . . .

The waiter brings the beer, sets the glasses down amid the moist streaks on the table. Suddenly, completely clearly, as it might occur to someone who has drunk nothing, a question rings out in Ivan's head: 'But where on earth can he be now, that little sailor? And that curly-headed accordionist?' And suddenly he is seized with pity for both of them. And, without knowing why, with pity, too, for his drinking companions. His chin begins to tremble and, half lying across the table, he holds out his arms to embrace them and can no longer see anything through his tears.

Before leaving, they drink the third bottle of vodka and go staggering out into the street, holding one another up. The night is full of stars. The snow crunches underfoot. Ivan slips and falls. The signalman picks him up with difficulty.

'It's nothing! It's nothing, Ivan! Don't worry. We'll take you home. You'll get there, don't worry . . .'

After that something strange occurs. Nikolaï turns off through a gateway. The signalman sits Ivan down on a bench, goes off in search of a taxi and never comes back. Ivan stands up with difficulty. 'I'll get there on my own,' he thinks. 'There's a shop next, then the District Committee, and after that I turn left . . .'

But on the corner, instead of seeing the four-storey block of flats and its familiar entrance gate, he sees a broad avenue with cars driving along it. He stops, baffled, leans against the wall of the building. Then he retraces his steps unsteadily, in retreat from this broad avenue that does not exist in Borissov. Yet these snowdrifts certainly exist in Borissov. He needs to skirt round them. And this bench and this fence also exist. Yes, that's it, all he has to do now is cross this courtyard . . . But at the end of the courtyard an improbable apparition rears up – a vast skyscraper, like a rocket, illuminated by thousands of windows. And once more he retraces his footsteps, slips, falls, picks himself up again, holding onto a tree covered in hoar-frost. Once more he heads for the familiar snowdrifts, and the bench, without realizing that he is not in Borissov but in Moscow, wandering round Kazan railway station, where he got off the train this morning.

*   *   *

88

Two vehicles pulled up almost simultaneously beside the snowdrift where Ivan lay. One of them, from the militia, was collecting drunks to take them to the sobering-up station; the other was an ambulance. The first of these was doing its midnight rounds, the second had been summoned by a kind-hearted pensioner, who from his window had seen Ivan lying on the ground. His *shapka* had flown off five yards away when he fell. None of the passers-by out late at night had taken a fancy to it. Who needs a lorry driver's battered old headgear? As he fell, Ivan had grazed his cheek on the edge of the bench, but the cold blood had solidified without even staining the snow.

A drowsy militiaman got down from the cabin of the van: a young nurse sprang out of the ambulance, with a coat thrown on over her white blouse. She bent over the prostrate body and exclaimed: 'Oh! This isn't our responsibility. What's the point of ringing us? He's a drunk! Any fool can see that. But they ring you up and say: "Come quick. There's someone on the ground, in the road . . . Maybe knocked down by a car. Or else a heart attack . . ." A likely story! You can smell him a mile off.'

The militiaman bent over as well, picked up the body by the collar and turned it over on its back.

'Well, we're certainly not going to take him. There's blood all over his face. A piss artist? Sure he's a piss artist. But there's a physical injury . . . It's down to you to treat him. It's not our job.'

'You've got a nerve, you have,' cried the nurse angrily. 'Treat him! He's going to throw up all over the ward. And who's going to clear up after him? It's hard enough finding cleaners as it is . . .'

'Well picking up people with physical injuries isn't our job, I'm telling you. He may croak in the van. Or under the shower. He could bleed to death in there.'

'What do you mean, bleed to death? Don't make me laugh!

From that little scratch? Here, take a look at it, this physical injury . . .'

The nurse crouched down, extracted a little phial of alcohol and a wad of cotton wool out of her satchel and wiped the scratch on Ivan's cheek.

'There. There's your "physical injury",' she said, showing the militiaman the cotton wool lightly stained with brown. 'It's not even bleeding.'

'Right. Well, as you've started treating him, you'd better finish the job. Pick him up and let's call it a day.'

'No chance! Picking up boozers is your job. Otherwise what's the point of having all your sobering-up stations?'

'What's the point? If we take him in now with his mug all bloody, tomorrow morning he's going to be howling: "The law did me over." Everyone knows the form these days. At the smallest bit of trouble, wham!, you get a story in the paper: "Violation of socialist legality". Oh yes! We've got *glasnost* now . . . Thanks to Gorbachev the whole place is swarming with rabble-rousers. Under Stalin they'd have soon banged you up . . . Right! If that's how it is, write me a certificate testifying that he's got a bloody head. Otherwise I'm not taking him.'

'But I don't have the right to make out a medical certificate until he's been examined.'

'Go ahead then. Examine him . . .'

'No chance. We don't have anything to do with drunks!'

The argument dragged on. The driver got down from the ambulance; the second militiaman emerged from the yellow 'Special Medical Service' van. He poked the body with his foot as it lay there and muttered: 'Why are you wasting your breath? He may have kicked the bucket already. Let me have a look.'

He bent over and very brutally applied pressure behind Ivan's ears with two fingers.

'Here, you want to remember this little dodge,' he laughed,

winking at the nurse. 'It's better than all your smelling salts. This'll waken the dead.'

In response to intolerable pain, Ivan opened wild eyes and gave a dull groan.

'Alive!' chuckled the militiaman. 'It'll take more than that to finish him off. He looks like he's lying under the streetlamp to get a tan. All right, Seryozha, I reckon we'd better pick him up. At all events we can't leave this man in the hands of these quacks. They do in more people than they cure.'

'And you're plaster saints, I suppose!' retorted the nurse, glad to have won her battle at last. 'I tell you, there was an article on sobering-up stations in *Pravda* the other day. When they bring a drunk in they empty his pockets. They steal his pay, his watch. They take everything . . .'

'Right, that's enough of that,' the militiaman cut in. 'We've had a bellyful as it is, what with Gorbachev and his speeches. Him and his *perestroika* are a pain in the neck . . .'

The nurse jumped into the ambulance, slammed the door and the vehicle drove off.

They lugged Ivan into the van and let him fall on the floor. One of the militiamen got behind the wheel, the other unbuttoned the top of Ivan's coat, searching for his papers. He took out a battered record of service, held it up to the light and began to decipher it. Suddenly he uttered a whistle of surprise.

'Oh my God, Seryozha, he's a Hero of the Soviet Union! And those sodding medics wouldn't take him off our hands! So now what are we going to do?'

'Well, what can we do? It makes no odds to us if he's a Hero of the Soviet Union or even a bloody cosmonaut. Our job's simple: we find him, we pick him up, we take him back, that's all. And at the station it's down to the officer to decide. Right, let's go. Close that fucking door, my feet are frozen already.'

*   *   *

91

Ivan had taken to drinking straight after his wife's death. He drank a lot, fiercely, without explaining it to himself, without repenting, without ever promising himself to stop. Borissov is a small town. Soon everyone knew about the Hero turned drunkard.

The head of the vehicle pool called Ivan in from time to time and lectured him indulgently, as if talking to a child who had done something silly.

'Listen, Dmitrich, this is not good at all. You've got another two years before you retire and you carry on like this. That's twice they've picked you up dead drunk in broad daylight. It's lucky the local militia know you, otherwise you'd soon have been sent to the sobering-up station. I know you have your troubles but you're not a finished man. And don't forget you're behind a wheel. You risk either knocking someone over or getting killed yourself. And look what a bad example you're setting the young people.'

They summoned him to the District Committee and also to the Veterans' Council, but in vain.

At the District Committee, Ivan listened to the Secretary's catalogue of reproaches and admonitions. Suddenly he interrupted him in a weary voice: 'That's enough footling nonsense, Nikolayich. You'd be better employed working out how to feed the people. Instead of which you talk a lot of rubbish – the Communist's duty, civic responsibility . . . It's a pain to listen to you!'

The Party Secretary burst out furiously: 'Your drinking makes you forget where you are, Hero! As a member of the Party, how can you say such things?'

Ivan rose to his feet, leaned across the table towards the Secretary and observed in a low, dry voice: 'Just now, I can do anything . . . Understood? And as for my Party card, I could chuck it right back at you, here on the table, if I chose!'

At the Veterans' Council the retired officers gathered there were looking forward with relish to some free entertainment.

Ivan disappointed them all. He offered no explanation or defence, and did not argue with his irate accusers. He sat there, nodding his head and even smiling. He thought: 'What's the point of offending these old men? Let them talk! Let them feel good. There's no malice in them, they're just bored. Look at that one, he's getting so worked up he's making his medals jangle. What a funny old bugger! He's turned himself out smart as anything. No trouble spared . . .'

The entertainment did not take place.

Towards 9 May, as if he were observing a self-imposed fast, Ivan stopped drinking. He ran a broom over the rooms that for a long time had looked uninhabited. He cleaned his best suit, polished his medals and his Gold Star with tooth powder, and waited for the pioneers. They usually came a few days before the Victory celebration, presented him with an invitation on a colourful card and, after stammering out their prepared message, bolted down the staircase shouting gleefully.

He spent nearly a week waiting for them. 'The little lads must have forgotten,' he thought. 'They've got other things on their minds. Well, all the better for me. It was tiring in the long run, telling the same stories year after year.'

But on 8 May he put on all his medals and went out. He wondered curiously: 'Why haven't they invited me? If they've invited someone else, who is it?'

He walked past the school twice but no one came out to meet him. Then he sat down in a square from which the entrance to the school could be seen. People walking past him greeted him with little disdainful smiles, as if to say: 'Aha! The Hero! You've been seen dead drunk under a bench . . .'

In his head, inevitably, he heard the echo of phrases from his talks in days gone by: 'Now then, my friends, just picture the scorching heat on the steppe in the summer of '42. In the distance Stalingrad is in flames and we're just a handful of soldiers . . .'

He kept turning to look at the school gate more and more often, was annoyed with himself, but could not overcome his curiosity. At length it opened wide and the stream of schoolchildren poured out into the street, shouting and squabbling. 'The lesson on remembrance and patriotism' was over. Then a soldier appeared in the doorway, escorted by a teacher. The soldier was holding three red carnations in his hand. Ivan went up to him in the alleyway. He was a young sergeant, the son of one of the drivers in their vehicle pool.

'Alexeï, you're demobbed already?' asked Ivan, with genial amazement.

'Since last autumn, Ivan Dmitrich. And after that I spent ages in hospital. I had a foot blown off. You can see the kind of clodhoppers I wear now.'

Ivan looked down. On one of the young sergeant's feet he was wearing a monstrously swollen orthopaedic ankle boot.

'And how's it going back there in Afghanistan? It's a funny thing but they never mention it in the papers now . . .'

'Well, what could they say about it? Back there we're in the shit up to our necks . . .'

'So, you've just come from the school like this?'

'Yes, they invited me to the lesson on patriotism.'

'So what did the children ask you?'

'They asked about the duty of internationalist soldiers and about the brotherhood of arms. And one scallywag at a desk in the back row stood up and said: "Please tell me, comrade staff-sergeant, how many mujahedin did you kill yourself?" Well, there you are . . . The artificial limbs they make for us are simply diabolical. When you walk down the street you have to grit your teeth. And when you take them off your boots are full of blood. It's as hard as . . . Well, Ivan Dmitrich, have a good holiday. Happy Victory Day! Here, look at these flowers. Take them, Dmitrich. You're a Hero, you deserve them. Give them to your wife . . . What? . . . But when? . . . Good God! That's terrible! I knew nothing about it. I've only been out of hospital for five days. Well, chin up, Ivan Dmitrich . . . And . . . Happy Victory Day! . . .'

A year later Ivan retired. The head of the vehicle pool heaved a sigh of relief. They bid him a solemn farewell; they presented him with a heavy grey marble writing set and an electronic watch. The watch Ivan sold almost immediately: vodka had gone up and his pension was barely adequate. No one wanted the writing set, not even for three roubles.

That year Gorbachev came to power. Ivan watched his speeches on television. It was the month of May, the time for his abstinence. This animated and garrulous man, Gorbachev, created a strange impression when he spoke, forever removing his glasses, putting them on again and cracking jokes: 'We must develop the system of vegetable plots,' he would say, waving his hands like a conjuror seeking to hypnotize his audience. 'You know, little gardens, little vegetable plots. Several million men among us want to become the owners of land but we, for the moment, cannot satisfy their demands . . .'

There were very few people then who suspected that what this whole scenario, all these 'vegetable plots', amounted to really was a magician's patter to lull people's vigilance. In Russia it was always necessary to act out this drama of humility as a preliminary to climbing onto the throne. Khrushchev performed folk dances in front of Stalin, Brezhnev feigned a heart attack in front of Kaganovich, Gorbachev did conjuring tricks in front of the old *mafiosi* of the Politburo, whom he had to overcome.

That year, as in the previous year, Ivan pulled himself together for several days. He did the housework in the flat, walked through the town wearing all his medals, visited the cemetery. The photo of Tatyana in its oval frame set in the monument had turned yellow, and the rains had caused it to warp. But to Ivan she seemed strangely alive.

As he passed by the town's wall of honour he saw they had already removed his own photo. All that remained was an empty metal frame and the stupid remnant of an inscription: 'Soviet Hero . . . from vehicle pool No. 1 . . .'

People did not forget that he was a Hero. For old time's sake the militia would bring him home when he was laid low by vodka. When he did not have enough money for his bottle at the shop, the assistant would give him credit.

Gradually his flat emptied. He sold the carpet he had bought in Moscow with Tatyana in the old days. He disposed of all the saleable furniture for almost nothing. Gorbachev's speech about little vegetable plots was the last transmission he watched: he swopped his television set for three bottles of vodka. He carried all this out with a casual unconcern that surprised even himself. He actually went as far as getting rid of the rings and earrings preserved in his wife's jewellery box, and several silver spoons.

One day in autumn he was unable to get hold of money for drinking. The cold wind kept his drinking companions at home; there was a new assistant working at the shop now; his neighbours laughed and slammed the door in his face when he tried to borrow three roubles. For some time he wandered through the cold, dirty streets, then went home and took his best suit, complete with all the gongs, out of the wardrobe. For a moment he studied the heavy gilded and silvered disks, fingering the cold metal, and removed the Order of the Red Banner of War. He did not have the courage to try to sell it in Borissov. People knew him too well here and no doubt no one would be tempted. He went through all his pockets, gathered together the small change and bought a ticket to Moscow. He sold his medal there for twenty-five roubles and got drunk.

After that he went to Moscow almost every week.

The one thing he never touched was his Gold Star. He knew he would never touch it.

So it was that when they went through his clothes at the sobering-up station in Moscow, they found two 'For Gallantry' medals and the Order of Glory second class, all wrapped in a scrap of crumpled newspaper. On it Ivan had written in ballpoint pen: 'ten roubles' for each medal, 'twenty-five roubles' for the Order, so as to avoid any mistakes in his drunken state – all the more because the sale would have to be made quickly in a dark corner. The duty officer informed the criminal investigation department of this find.

In the morning they let him go. He walked along slowly, not really knowing where he was going, taking in gulps of fresh, blue air through his parched lips, his eyes screwed up against the dazzling March sun. He only desired one thing: to buy a bottle of alcohol quickly and, without a glass, drinking from the neck, choking on it, to ingest a few lifesaving draughts. He felt through his pockets and took out the medals and the Order, unable to believe his luck. 'They haven't taken them,' he thought happily. 'So? Don't they search you any more at that station . . . ?'

The militiaman detailed to catch Ivan red-handed made his move too fast. Ivan had just unwrapped his treasure. The dealer had not yet taken out his money. He saw the militiaman in plain clothes looming up in front of them and began yawning in a bored manner. 'Well I never, little father, so those are war medals that you've got there! No, that doesn't interest me. That's a recipe for ending up in the slammer, you know. It's not my scene.'

The militiaman swore in frustration, flashed his red card and indicated to Ivan a car that was waiting for them.

That evening he went home to Borissov. At the police station they had decided not to pursue it. To begin with he had not been caught red-handed. Besides, he was a Hero, after all. He travelled back on an overcrowded train. Sweating heavily and dazed with exhaustion from queueing in Moscow, people were carrying great bundles of provisions. March 8, International Women's Day, was drawing near. Standing there, squeezed against a creaking door, Ivan was absently drumming on the smooth, round medals in his pocket and thinking: 'If only someone would speak to me . . . There they all are, with their sour faces . . . Their mouths shut tight and their bags crammed with fodder . . . It'd be good to kick the bucket here and now. They'd bury me and it'd be all over and done with . . . Spring's on the way now, the earth's good and soft already. It thaws quickly . . .'

From Moscow they sent a report on Ivan to the District Committee of the Party. They recounted the episode at the sobering-up station and the trafficking in medals. The matter went all the way up to the Party's Central Committee. 'How's this! The Hero of Stalingrad has become an alcoholic who sells his war medals! And just as we're coming up to the for-tieth anniversary of the Victory!' Furthermore, Gorbachev's conjuring tricks were turning out not to be conjuring tricks at all; heads were beginning to roll. It was Year One of the Gorbachevian Revolution.

From the Central Committee they had telephoned to the Regional Committee, from the Regional Committee to the District Committee. The reproaches snowballed. The Party District Committee's Secretary, having received a warning shot, nervously dialled the number of the Regional Military Committee. Ivan was summoned to it by a simple notice. The officer who saw him instructed him to hand over his army documents and his Hero of the Soviet Union certificate. 'They're going to stick another little bit of anniversary scrap iron on me,' thought Ivan.

Without even opening the army papers, the officer handed them back to Ivan; the Hero's certificate he tossed into the safe with a brisk gesture and slammed the thick little door shut.

'For the time being your certificate will stay with us,' he said drily.

And in grave tones he added: 'In accordance with the instructions of the Party District Committee.'

In a futile impulse, Ivan gestured towards the safe, as if reaching for the little door. But the officer stood up and shouted into the corridor: 'Sergeant, escort this citizen to the exit.'

At the District Committee Ivan thrust aside the switchboard operator who tried to bar his way and burst into the Party Secretary's office. The latter was talking on the telephone and when Ivan accosted him with a shout he put his hand over the receiver and said in a low voice: 'I'll have you thrown out by a militiaman.'

Having finished his conversation he gave Ivan a nasty look and intoned: 'We shall be addressing a request to the higher authorities, Comrade Demidov, to seek the revocation of your award as Hero of the Soviet Union. That's all. This interview is at an end. I shall detain you no further.'

'It wasn't you that gave me that award and it won't be you that takes it away from me,' muttered Ivan dully.

'Precisely. It's not my responsibility. It is within the competence of the Supreme Soviet. That's where they'll review whether a depraved alcoholic has the moral right to wear the Gold Star.'

Ivan greeted these words with a heavy shout of laughter.

'No. Not the Star. You won't take that away from me, you gang of bastards. Even the Fritzes at the camp never found it on me. Though they searched me enough times! I screwed it into the palm of my hand. They shouted: "Hands up!" And I spread my fingers but it stayed in place. Look! Like this!'

And with a bitter smile Ivan showed the Secretary the

five points of the Star embedded in his palm. The Secretary was silent.

'That's how it is, citizen chief,' repeated Ivan, who was no longer smiling. 'What? You didn't know I'd been a prisoner of war? Well, no one knew. If it had come out I'd have been rotting in a camp at Kolyma long ago. Go on! Telephone the Military Committee. Let those rats do a bit of research. They might find a little two-month gap in '44. And as for the Star, you'll never take it from me. You'll have to rob my corpse for it . . .'

Ivan could not bring himself to go home. He dreaded seeing again the empty coatstand in the corridor, the grey pile of dirty linen, the washbasin yellow with rust. For a long time he walked about in the muddy spring streets and, when he noticed someone coming towards him, turned aside. Then he made his way round the furniture factory, beyond which there was already an expanse of open country, and emerged onto a waste land that smelled of damp snow. Close by, beneath a layer of spongy ice, a stream murmured softly. On the sloping verge the snow had already melted in places, uncovering dark, swollen earth. This earth gave way underfoot in a soft and supple manner. And once more it seemed to Ivan not frightening but warm and tender, like river clay.

'I've lasted too long,' thought Ivan. 'I should have gone sooner. They'd have buried me with full honours.' He realized that throughout that time he had been hoping for a brutal and unexpected end, an end that happened of its own accord, sweeping everything into the void: the dead flat, the dark entrance where drunkards lingered, himself. That was why he was destroying himself with such abandon, almost joyfully. But the end did not come.

When dusk was beginning to fall Ivan went back into the town, walked along the streets once more – the 'Progress' Cinema, the District Committee, the militia. Beside the

Gastronom shop there was a long, serpentine queue. One of the men at the end of the line dropped a bag full of empty bottles. He started picking up the pieces, cut his fingers and swore in a weary, monotonous voice.

'If only I could buy half a litre and down it first . . . otherwise I don't think I'll have the courage,' thought Ivan. But he had nothing to pay with. 'Right, I'll try to find the sleeping pills. But it'll have to be done later, or else the neighbours will suspect something.'

And he continued wandering. When night came the cold made the stars glitter. The ice-bound snow crackled underfoot. But there was already a smell of spring on the wind. Close to his home Ivan lifted his head – almost all the windows were already dark. It was dark, too, in the courtyard beside the block of flats. Dark and silent. In the silence Ivan heard the light crunch of the snow beneath the feet of a stray dog. Happy at the thought of being able to stroke it and look into its anxious, tender eyes, he turned round. The night wind was causing a ball of crumpled newspaper to roll along the ground . . .

Ivan went in through the main door and was preparing to climb up to his flat on the third floor; but remembered he should look at the mail. He hardly ever opened his box for weeks at a time, knowing that if something was dropped in it, it was almost certainly by mistake. His daughter sent him three cards a year: on Soviet Army Day, his birthday and Victory Day. The first two dates were already past, the third was still a long way off. This time he found a letter. Only the upper floors were lit and where the box was almost total darkness reigned. 'Moscow', Ivan made out on the envelope. 'It must be the bill from the sobering-up station. Hell's bells! They're quick off the mark . . . That's the capital for you . . .'

In the course of his wanderings through the town he had had time to collect his thoughts. He had been thinking about it all with surprising detachment, as if it concerned someone else. He recalled where there was a razor amid the chaos in the kitchen; and in which of the drawers in the chest the pills were kept. He was no longer on good terms with his neighbours on the same floor. Which is why he decided to slip the note asking for someone to come and see him under the door of the flat below, where Zhora, a robust warehouseman, lived. He got on well with him and occasionally they had a drink together. 'It's all right, he's tough. He's not one to be scared,' thought Ivan. 'That's important. Someone else might have a heart attack . . .'

As he climbed up the stairs he was fingering his neck, trying to find where the blood throbbed most strongly. 'That must be it, the carotid. Oho! It's really pounding away there. The main thing's to hit it first time off. Otherwise you're going to be running around like a chicken with its throat half cut!'

At the flat he took out the razor and found the sleeping pills. On a piece of paper he wrote: 'Zhora, come to number 84. It's important.' Then he went and slipped the note under the door.

Back at home, he made a tour of the flat, glanced at a photo in a wooden frame: Tatyana and himself, still very young, and in the background palm trees and the misty outline of the mountains. Then, he filled a glass with water from the tap and began to swallow the pills one after the other.

Soon Ivan felt a thick fog that muffled all sounds, revolving slowly in his head. He opened the razor and, as if to shave himself, lifted his chin.

At that moment he remembered he had slammed the door shut and that he needed to leave it on the latch, otherwise Zhora would not be able to get in. His mind was still functioning and this afforded him an absurd satisfaction. In the entrance hall he took the medals, wrapped in an old piece of newspaper, out of his coat pocket, together with the letter from the Moscow sobering-up station. He tossed the medals into a drawer and, holding the letter up to the light, opened the envelope unhurriedly. There was nothing official there. The page, covered in regular feminine handwriting, began with these words: 'Dear Dad! It's been a long time since I last wrote to you, but you've no idea what life is like in Moscow . . .'

Ivan picked up the envelope and read the sender's address with difficulty: 'Moscow, 16 Litovsky Avenue, Flat 37, Demidova o.I.' Feverishly, muddling up lines of text that were already growing blurred, his eye seized upon fragments of sentences: 'I've got to know a nice young man . . . We're thinking of getting married in July . . . His parents would like to meet you. Come for the May celebrations . . . You can stay with us for a week or two . . .'

Ivan could never recall the very last sentence in the letter, even though he saw it absolutely clearly, even repeated it, as it seemed to him, whispering, 'The bells are ringing in Moscow . . . The bells are ringing . . . And who's going to hear them?'

It was not until the afternoon that Ivan came to. He opened his eyes, then screwed them up against the blinding sunlight beating on the windowpanes. He was lying on the floor. Above him crouched Zhora, shaking him by the shoulder.

'Dmitrich, Dmitrich! Wake up now, you bloody Veteran! You're not half a boozer! Where did you get plastered like that? No, don't shut your eyes, you'll nod off again. Why did you send for me? What's this urgent business, then? To wake you up? Eh? D'you think I've got nothing better to do than come and sober you up?'

Listening to him and scarcely grasping the import of his words, Ivan smiled. Then just as Zhora was preparing to go, Ivan forced open his swollen lips and asked softly: 'Zhora, let me have five roubles. I'll pay you back next pension day.'

Zhora whistled softly to himself, got up and thrust his hands into his pockets.

'My hat, Dmitrich, you've got a nerve! Now you've found yourself a pioneer who's done his good deed for the day, I suppose you'll be wanting me to bring you the occasional bottle and give you the titty to suck . . .'

Then he glanced around the shabby, empty flat and at Ivan, his thin face devoured by his beard, and said in a conciliatory voice: 'Look, I haven't got five roubles. Here's three. That'll be enough to take care of your hangover. Yesterday at the Gastronom they had a strong one in at two roubles seventy a bottle. The lads say it's all right . . .'

Feeling a little better, Ivan doused his head pleasurably under the cold tap for a long time, then went out into the springtime street and made his way unhurriedly towards the shop, smiling at the warm sunshine.

On his return he cooked some noodles in a saucepan. He ate them slowly, along with some cheap tinned fish. After the meal he emptied a whole packet of washing powder into the bathtub, gathered up all the linen and clothes and did a great, clumsy wash, the way men do.

When Ivan caught sight of Olya at the railway station, in the middle of the dense, teeming crowd, she had changed so much it took his breath away. As they made their way towards the metro he could not get used to the idea that this svelte young woman was his daughter. Everything about her was so simple and naturally harmonious – neat light-grey shoes, black stockings, a full jacket with broad shoulders.

'My goodness, Olya! You've turned into a real Westerner!' he said, shaking his head.

She laughed.

'That's right, Dad. "When in Rome do as the Romans do!" I can't help it. You know what big fish I have to deal with. Only yesterday I was just having my last session with a capitalist who's got factories in seven different countries . . . With people like that we have to look reasonably presentable or they don't sign our contracts.'

'And look at me, a real peasant. You must be ashamed to walk beside me.'

'Nonsense, Dad. What are you saying? Not at all! Your Star alone is worth all the rest of them. And as to clothes, don't worry. Tomorrow we'll sort things out. You see, you couldn't visit Alexeï's parents in that suit. And, most of all, you need a new shirt.'

Ivan actually thought his shirt was the best thing he had on. He had bought it some days before his departure and trying it on had cheered him up – he had felt rejuvenated and dashing, like in the old days. What pleased him particularly was that the shirt did not constrict his neck; although he buttoned it up right to the top.

During the past few weeks he had tidied up the flat and one warm April day had even washed the windows. He washed them slowly, delighting in the freshness and lightness of the air coming into the rooms . . .

On the following day Olya took him into a big shop where a sickly sweet, suffocating scent hung on the air.

'You know, Dad, we could have bought everything at a Beriozka, of course. I've got vouchers for that. But, you see, first of all, my parents-in-law are such snobs that nothing impresses them. And secondly, your Star wouldn't look right on an imported suit. So we'll find something made at home but good quality.'

Wearing this navy-blue suit that fitted him well, Ivan looked in the mirror and did not recognize himself.

'There we are,' joked Olya, 'a real retired general. Now we'll go and buy a couple of shirts and some ties.'

Back at home she tormented him by tying and untying his tie and searching for the best place to fix the Star.

'Leave it, Olya,' Ivan finally begged. 'It's fine like that. You're fussing over me as if I were a young lady. Anyone would think I was the one getting married . . .'

'Oh, if only you knew, Dad,' sighed Olya. 'Nothing's simple. You have to think of everything, plan everything. You've no idea of the circles these big fish move in. They're forever travelling abroad. Their flat's like a museum. They drink coffee from antique china and mix with other people like that: diplomats, writers, ministers . . . Hold on a minute, don't move! I'm going to take a little tuck here, while you're wearing it, and I'll stitch it up afterwards; otherwise the shirt will gape and that won't look very nice . . . You see, they're really the cream of Moscow society. Alyosha's father went to college with Gorbachev at Moscow State and they're still on first-name terms. Just think! Right, one last try and I'll leave you in peace. Goodness, Dad, you're ever so thin. You're all skin and bone. I suppose you can't find anything in the shops in Borissov . . . There. That's it. Take a look in the mirror. A real superman! Tomorrow we'll go and buy you some suitable shoes. Then I'll take you out. No. The Star's too high up. Hold on. I'll move it down a bit . . .'

The visit to the future parents-in-law was due to take place on 9 May, Victory Day. Olya had thought this date an excellent choice. They would be showing some documentary or other on television. Her father would recall the old days and would talk about his memories. This would be a good topic of conversation. They certainly wouldn't be discussing the latest Paris exhibition with him . . .

It was true. Nothing was totally simple.

When she had written to her father that the wedding was planned for July she had been slightly anticipating events. Alexeï talked about this marriage rather evasively. His parents, for their part, were very kind to her. But in their very worldly kindness Olya scented the risk of all her plans collapsing. Indeed it would not even be a collapse as such. Simply a friendly smile, a sweet and mildly surprised look from beneath a raised eyebrow. 'But, you poor little idiot, how could you ever hope to take your place in our milieu?'

She had noticed this smile for the first time when she had told them she was working as an interpreter at the Centre. Alexeï's mother smiled absently, stirring her coffee with a little spoon. Meanwhile his father grinned broadly and exclaimed in somewhat theatrical tones: 'Ha! Well I never!' And they exchanged rapid glances.

'Do they know exactly what my work is?' wondered Olya, in torment. 'Of course they do. But perhaps they don't give a damn? Or do they put up with me on account of Alyosha? Because they don't want to upset him? Surely even he must know . . .'

Of late this marriage had become an obsession with her. It seemed to her that if she succeeded in getting Alexeï to marry her it would not only be a new era but a completely different life. Good-bye to snow-covered Yassenievo, good-bye to that room in the system-built block of flats! Now it would be the centre of Moscow and a prestige building and an entrance hall with a caretaker and her husband's official car parked under the window. All this assembly-line espionage would come to an end; Alexeï's parents would find her honourable employment in some export trade department. And perhaps Alexeï would be posted abroad, to an embassy; she would go with him and it would be her turn to pass through those customs barriers at Sheremetevo, from beyond which her clients generally waved her good-bye. Or rather not through the same barrier but straight in at the diplomats' entrance.

She had talked to Svetka about all this one day in winter. The latter, spinning her hula-hoop furiously, said to her: 'The main thing, Olya, you know, is not to let yourself go. You haven't got there yet. Do you remember Chekhov's story, "The Eel" . . . There it is, already caught by the gills but it gives a flick of its tail and, hey presto! it heads for the open sea . . . Now, listen carefully to my advice: get them to invite your father. He's a Hero, after all. Get him to put on all his medals and take him along to your future parents-in-law. So it'll be a bit like a family gathering already . . . Well, what's embarrassing about that? The only embarrassing thing in the whole world is trying to put your trousers on over your head. Go for it! I know them, these little diplomats . . . they're as slippery as eels. Don't believe it's happened till you've got the stamp on your passport.'

She stopped spinning and the hula-hoop slipped lazily to her feet. Picking up the tape measure she measured her waist.

'Oh, drat! I just can't work off all those goodies from the New Year! That's right, laugh. Go ahead and make fun of a poor, sick, old woman. I find you a fiancé and you don't even thank me! Once you're married you won't know me any more. You'll be driving around in a limousine with your little hubby. But I don't care. By then my Vovka will have become a general in Afghanistan. We'll be just as good as you . . . Right, I must get spinning again, otherwise the capitalists won't love me any more . . .'

In the morning Olya went off to work and Ivan spent the whole day strolling about Moscow. He felt like an impressive retired officer, ambling with a measured tread along the springtime streets. The passers-by eyed his Gold Star and people gave up their seats to him on the metro. Sitting on a bench in the park, he would have liked to get into conversation with someone and quite by chance mention his daughter. Here's how it had happened. The two of them had been simple workers and their daughter was such a high flyer that now she was working with foreign diplomats.

He would have liked to tell how they had bought his suit, talk about her future parents-in-law, about the leather wallet she had given him. Within its fragrant folds he had found a hundred-rouble note. 'That's for your meals, Dad,' Olya had explained. 'I don't have time to cook lunch for you . . .'

One day, walking past the Bolshoï Theatre, he had overheard a conversation between two women who had a provincial look about them.

'No chance, I've asked. Because of Victory Day they're only selling tickets to Veterans. And foreigners, of course, who pay in currency.'

'Maybe you need to grease the administrator's palm,' said the other one.

'Oh yes. Then he'll sell us some! Very likely. I expect he's desperate for our crumpled old roubles!'

Near the Bolshoï box office, across the square from the Kremlin, Ivan saw an enormous buzzing crowd, seething angrily. It began in the tunnel leading from the metro, stretched up the staircase and spilled out into the open towards the glass doors of the box office.

'It's always like this,' grumbled one woman. 'You come to Moscow once in a lifetime and what happens? All the tickets go to the Veterans!'

'What do you mean – the Veterans?' someone else cut in. 'Everything's put on one side to be sold at three times the price.'

'That's all poppycock. What they're after is foreign currency. There's no oil left, so they're selling culture!' shouted a third from the heart of the throng.

Unbuttoning his raincoat so his Star could be seen, Ivan threaded his way towards the ticket office. 'I'll give Olya a surprise,' he thought happily. 'I'll come home and say in an offhand way: "Why don't we go to the theatre, this evening? To the Bolshoï, perhaps?" She'll be amazed. "But how? We'll never get any tickets." And then, with a wave of my wand, "Never get any?" says I. "Look, here they are."'

Outside the crowd was pressing against a metal barrier,

beside which stood three militiamen. Seeing the Hero's Star, they opened the barrier a little and let Ivan through towards the ticket office. There, in front of the doors that were still shut, a few dozen Veterans had gathered. Ivan studied the rows of decorations on the lapels of their jackets and even noticed a couple of Gold Stars on one of them. Several of them looked as if they had been waiting for a long while and, to pass the time, they were telling one another about their war experiences. The sky had been overcast since the morning and now damp snow was falling, brought on by an icy wind. People shivered, turned up their coat collars. Near the door stood a disabled man in a worn overcoat all hunched up, supported on his single leg.

'What ho, the old guard!' called out Ivan. 'What are we waiting here for? Aren't there any more tickets?'

'We're waiting to be called,' came the reply. 'At midday they'll count us again and let us in.'

And indeed at noon precisely the door opened and a sleepy woman with a discontented air announced: 'There are a hundred and fifty tickets on sale. The rule is two tickets per person, which means one for the Veteran and one for a member of his family. Those who've got queue numbers form a line. The others, go to the back.'

Large snowflakes were falling and a bitter wind was blowing. Not far away, emerging from the gates of the Kremlin, came a cavalcade of official cars, as long and gleaming as pianos. And there stood the crowd, thrust back by the barriers and the militiamen, a crowd awaiting a miracle and eyeing the Veterans with fierce jealousy, as they formed a line.

'Thirty-one, thirty-two, thirty-three . . .' mumbled the drowsy woman in haughty tones.

And the old men, giving a start, bustled up and hastily took their places in the column.

'Is this what we spilt our blood for?' called out a mocking voice in front of Ivan.

Looking more closely Ivan saw the face of a man of the people crinkled up in a smile. It was the disabled man who stood several places in front of him. The face struck him as familiar.

Ivan ended up as number sixty-two. He received two tickets for *The Stone Guest*. Emerging from the crowd, he went into the tunnel and headed for the metro. Passing a dark corner near some broken-down vending machines, he once more noticed the disabled Veteran. Confronting him were two smartly dressed young men, passing remarks at him while interrupting one another. Ivan stopped and pricked up his ears. Grasping the old man by the lapel, one of them barked at him sneeringly: 'Listen, Grandpa, don't try to be clever with us. We don't want the prices to go sky high, do we? You always sell them for five roubles. Why are you pissing us about? Take ten and bugger off and buy a bottle. You're never going to find a mug who'll give you fifteen, you old villain. They're not even in the stalls.'

'Well in that case, I'm not selling them. You can take it or leave it,' replied the Veteran.

He swung round on his crutches and tried to move away. But one of them pushed him towards the vending machines and seized his collar.

'Now listen to me, you flaming Hero of Borodino. I'm going to smash your flaming crutches for you. You'll have to crawl home.'

Ivan went up to them and asked in conciliatory tones: 'Now then, lads! What are you bothering this old soldier for?'

One of the fellows, rolling his chewing gum around in his mouth, took a step towards Ivan.

'Are you looking for a pair of crutches too, Grandpa?'

And he gave Ivan a careless shove with his shoulder.

'That's enough. Leave it, Valera!' the other one intervened. 'Let them go to hell, them and their Victory! Look, that one's a Hero of the Soviet Union. Let's go. Here comes the law.'

And then they swaggered off towards the metro.

Ivan held out his hand to the man on crutches. Shaking his hand in return, the latter, half embarrassed and half mischievously, said: 'Well, I recognized you straightaway, just now in the queue; but I didn't make myself known to you. So fancy that. You've gone up in the world with your tie and your Star . . . You must be a colonel at least, Vanya . . .'

'You're joking! I'm a general, old boy! Now I remember your surname well enough. But I've forgotten your first name. Sasha? Yes, of course. Alexander Semyonov. It comes back to me now. As if I could forget those great big ears of yours . . . Do you remember, we were always pulling your leg about them? We said you'd have to have a gas mask made to measure. And then the sergeant used to tease you: "Could you just tune into your radar, Sasha, and find out if the Fritzes are coming over on a bombing raid?" But what about your leg? Where did you lose it? If I remember correctly, it wasn't serious, just a scratch. Back in the ranks we even used to say you'd done it yourself!'

'You've no business to say that, Vanyusha. Look. What happened to me I wouldn't wish on my worst enemy. I'll tell you about it, but come to my place. We'll have a chat over a glass or two. I can't stay here long, all the militia know me. They keep moving me on, as if I had the plague! Don't worry, you'll have time to get back to your Yassenievo. Come on. It's my treat. I live in a *kommunalka* just round the corner.'

In the little room there was a touching sense of order.

'Look, Vanyush, they'd hardly finished butchering me when my wife left me. The way it happened . . . you see . . . was it all started with one toe. It was smashed up by a bit of shrapnel. They applied a tourniquet; but, good God, it was so cold – do you remember? – minus 40, and the leg froze. Then gangrene set in. They amputated my foot . . . They look again and it's already gone black further up. Then they cut it below the knee and it's started to rot above the knee. They cut it still higher, just leaving a stump they can fix an artificial leg to. It didn't work. So then they took it back just below the stomach . . . But what's the good of dredging all that up? Come on, Vanya, let's drink to the Victory!'

'Well I never! Me and the lads told all kinds of stories about you . . . There we were in the trench, you know, frozen to the marrow. Your name would come up and we'd say things like: "Just think, that bastard Semyonov . . . His toe was buggered up and now he's tucked up in bed with his wife under a warm quilt . . ." So that was the truth of it . . .'

'Yes, Vanyush. Believe me, I'd rather have had five years in the trenches than this. And I'd have been happy to spend all my life single. From the age of twenty . . . And now that's it. It's all over. You know at the hospital they were bringing us in by the wagonload, in whole trainloads. They had just enough time to disembark us. And, of course, they were hacking us about in double-quick time. Do you know, they severed all the nerves at the base of my stomach. It was just as if they'd castrated me. What woman would have wanted me after that?'

Semyonov switched on the television.

'Oh, look. Misha Gorbachev's on again. I like him a lot, that joker. He's a smooth talker and it's all off the cuff. Now Brezhnev, towards the end, was quite tongue-tied; you couldn't help feeling sorry for him. Even though, when all's said and done, he was an absolute bastard. When you think, he made himself a Hero of the Soviet Union three times over! All those medals he stuck on himself. While all I've got is one medal – for the defence of Moscow – plus all that anniversary ironmongery. And my pension's eighty roubles . . . !'

'So how on earth do you survive?' asked Ivan in amazement.

'I survive because I've got the knack for it. I've a strong enough grip to make me the envy of anyone. It just happened to be today that I got myself stuck with those two idiots. Normally it goes like clockwork. If you're a Veteran, especially one on crutches, they give you tickets without your having to queue. You've hardly walked away from the box office and people come running after you. "Sell us your tickets." They'll take them off you at any price you like. And I owe something else to Gorbachev. He passed the dry law, but how can people do without vodka? After seven in the evening people will part with twenty-five roubles for a ten-rouble bottle without batting an eyelid. Most of the hotel doormen know me: I do a good trade with them. Take a look at my stock, Vanya.'

Semyonov bent over on his chair and dragged a great dusty suitcase out from under the bed. Inside it, tightly packed together, were rows of bottles of all shapes and sizes, with labels of many colours.

'So you see, Vanyush, there's no need to hold back. Don't be shy. I've enough here for a whole regiment!'

But Ivan was no longer drinking. He already felt a pleasant and joyful numbness: already all the objects in this modest room radiated a warm well-being. He became voluble, talked about Stalingrad, the hospital, Tatyana. Semyonov was an excellent listener, did not interrupt him, made comments at the right moment and at the right moment expressed astonishment. In his bitter and turbulent life he had contrived to learn how to listen to people attentively. Everyone can tell stories but listening intelligently and without upstaging the speaker . . . now that is an art in itself!

Finally and without managing to conceal his delight, Ivan remarked: 'And as for me, Sasha, I'm not here in Moscow for the celebrations. I'm here to marry off my daughter. Yes, my dear fellow, just that. "Come to Moscow, Dad. My fiancé's parents want to meet you." When you have to, you have to. "And their family," she says, "are really people from the top drawer: some in the diplomatic corps, others in ministries." She's fixed me up very well, you see. I arrived here in an ancient suit I bought long ago in the days of old roubles.'

'And your daughter, Vanyush, where does she work?' asked Semyonov, neatly opening a tin of sardines.

Unable to conceal his pride but with offhand joviality, Ivan replied: 'Well, you know, my daughter's a very high flyer, Sasha. You could say that she's in the diplomatic world, too. It's such a shame that her mother didn't live to see her married. It'd have been a real thrill for her. Where she works is the International Trade Centre. You've heard of it?'

'Of course I know it! It's over by the Trekhgorka textile works near the river. Grey skyscrapers, just like America. You'd think you were in New York. So what does she do there?'

'How can I explain? Well, let's say an industrialist or a financier arrives, you see. He comes to sign a contract, to sell us some stuff; well, my daughter meets him, and translates everything our people say to him. In fact, she goes everywhere with him. And do you know how many foreign tongues she knows, Sasha?'

Ivan began to count them off but Semyonov was already listening somewhat absently, simply nodding his head from time to time and murmuring: 'Mm, mm . . .'

'Of course it's a tiring job, that goes without saying,' continued Ivan. 'Everything's planned to the last minute: conversations, negotiations. And what's more, night duty sometimes. But on the other hand, as I'm always telling her, you're not forever being sprayed with sawdust and there's no stink of petrol. And the pay's really good. I never earned that, not even when I was driving lorries long distance.'

Semyonov was silent as he absently poked with his fork at a little gleaming fish on his plate. Then he glanced uneasily at Ivan and, as if he were talking to someone else, muttered: 'You know, Vanya, it's a filthy business, if the truth be told.'

Ivan was dumbfounded.

'Filthy? What do you mean by that?'

'By that I mean, Vanyush, that . . . but don't be angry . . . I have to tell you . . . it's not their tongues those interpreters use for their work there. They use something else. That's why they're well paid.'

'Oh, Sasha! You shouldn't have drunk wine after vodka. Mixing the two's confused your brain. You're talking nonsense. It's laughable listening to you.'

'Don't listen if you don't want to. But the fact is I'm telling you the truth. And what's more, I'm not drunk at all. Down there, buried in your countryside, you know nothing. But I traipse all over Moscow with my crutches, through all the entrance gates; so they can't fool me. "Night duty". Pull the other one! Those businessmen have their way with the interpreters. They're there to pleasure them!'

'That's filthy gossip! So are you saying they're all prostitutes?'

'You can call it what you like. There are prostitutes in business on their own account. The militia hounds them from pillar to post. And then there are the others, the official ones, if you like. They're real interpreters, with diplomas, work permits, salary, the lot. By day they interpret and by night they service the capitalists in return for dollars.'

Semyonov was growing heated, he had a tousled and angry air. 'He's not drunk,' thought Ivan. 'And suppose what he says were true . . .'

And with a forced laugh he said: 'But Sasha, why the devil would the State go in for this nasty business?'

They began arguing again. With the feeling that something inside him was dying, Ivan realized that Semyonov was speaking the truth. And in his fear of believing him he jumped up, knocking over his glass, and with a hoarse shout grabbed hold of the man. He let go at once, so pitiful and light did his crippled body feel. Semyonov began yelling: 'You idiot, don't you understand? I'm trying to open your eyes! You strut about like a peacock with your shining Star. You don't understand that we've been had. We'll go together tomorrow. I'll show you this "night duty". I know one of the blokes in the cloakroom at the Intourist Hotel. He'll let us in . . . Yes, I promise you, they'll let us in, you'll see. I'll go without crutches, I'll take a stick. Here, take a look at this artificial leg I have . . .'

Semyonov scrambled off the chair onto the floor, rummaged under the bed and pulled out a metal leg with a huge black leather shoe. It seemed to Ivan as if he were living through a horrible and absurd dream. Semyonov let himself fall back on the bed and began to fit on his false leg, calling out: 'I'm only a half-portion. What damned good am I to anyone? They gave me the false leg free. If you wear it for a day your stomach bleeds all week. But for you, Vanya, I'll put it on. Tomorrow you'll see, I'll show you what your Star's worth . . . Under a warm quilt with my wife, you said . . . Ha ha ha!'

The cloakroom attendant let them settle down in a dark corner, hidden behind the dusty fronds of a palm tree growing in a large wooden container. From there could be seen the lifts, a small part of the restaurant and, through the dark French windows, the rear courtyard filled with refuse bins from the kitchen. Also visible were the two panels of the sliding doors to the inner entrance hall that opened automatically. That evening, possibly because of the wet snow, these doors were not working properly. They kept opening and closing all the time, with a mindless mechanical obedience, even when no one came near them.

Ivan was sitting beside Semyonov behind the palm tree, on the polished wooden planks that concealed the radiators. Semyonov was leaning sideways with his rigid leg stretched out. From time to time he gave explanations to Ivan in a low voice: 'There you see, in the basement behind the cloakroom, they have a *valyutka*, a currency bar. It's reserved for capitalists. And the girls, of course. You see that couple there walking towards the lift. And there, look at that tight-fitting dress. She's going to go with him. Ten minutes' work and she'll pocket what you used to earn in a month driving lorries.'

Ivan saw people coming and going who were unusual not only in their language and clothes but even in the way they moved.

Silently the lift doors opened and closed. A very young girl ran up to the cloakroom miaowing like a cat: 'You wouldn't have a packet of Marlboro, would you?'

'He trades, that one. He's no fool,' Semyonov explained to Ivan. 'She doesn't want to spend her currency, and maybe she hasn't earned it yet. She's very young . . .'

A large, dazzling woman sailed past, her bosom opulent beneath a fine knit dress. She walked on heels so high and pointed that her calves looked as if they were tensed with cramp. A young man in an elegant suit, a newspaper in his hand, stopped near the cloakroom desk. He exchanged a few offhand words with the attendant, glancing now at people emerging from the lifts, now at those entering the hotel. 'That one's from the KGB,' whispered Semyonov.

Ivan was wearied by the uninterrupted parade of faces and the mechanical creaking of the malfunctioning door. The blonde woman in the tight dress emerged from the lift and made for the cloakroom. 'Job done,' thought Ivan. The woman put on some lipstick in front of the mirror and headed for the exit. Absently he watched her go.

At that moment Ivan saw Olya.

She was walking beside a tall man, whose face Ivan did not have time to notice, such was the fascination with which he was staring at his daughter. Olya was talking to her companion, relaxed and natural. Semyonov nudged Ivan with his elbow and murmured something to him. Ivan heard nothing. He felt a horrible tensing inside himself and a salty taste tightening his jaws. He understood he ought to react, leap up, cry out, but he could not. When he began to hear again he caught a remark of Semyonov's: 'They're talking German, Ivan, can you hear?'

At the same moment the lift doors began to slide shut behind Olya and her companion. Reflected in the mirror in the cabin, Ivan saw a man's face with short grey hair, neatly trimmed. The lift doors closed smoothly.

Ivan tried to get up but was overcome with such a fit of trembling that his knees gave way. And once more he felt a salty lump in his throat. He had never before experienced such a painful, almost physical pang. He did not realize that what he was suffering from at this moment was a kind of jealousy.

Semyonov tugged at his sleeve, exclaiming in a muted voice: 'Vanya, Vanya, what is it? What's the matter with you? You've gone as white as a sheet . . .'

Stunned, Ivan gazed at him without seeing him and, unable to control a quivering at the corner of his mouth, breathed softly: 'That's my daughter.'

Four

'He's called Wilfried Almendinner ... No, not "Almendinner", what am I saying? Almendinger ... There's a surname for you! A real tongue-twister! We're going to take a great interest in him. Svetlana was supposed to be looking after him. But she's away on sick leave, you see. As to conversation, don't worry. To begin with, your German is perfectly adequate, and in any case he speaks Russian. He was here in the war. He was taken prisoner in the Ukraine and learned the language while they were rebuilding Leningrad. I'm telling you this, Olya, to give you a certain amount of background, so you can prepare yourself a little psychologically. But when you're talking to him, of course, you're not supposed to know that. In any case you know your business and you don't need me to remind you of it.'

Vitaly Ivanovich took a cigarette from the packet and lit it. He had a weary and disappointed air. Ever since the winter he had been looking forward to the blissful torpor that awaited him on the beach at the KGB's holiday home beside the Black Sea. And suddenly everything was turned upside down, the spring and summer holidays had been put back to the autumn and the order had been given to prepare for the International Festival of Youth and Students.

'They're all going to be gathering here, the whole pro-communist rabble,' Vitaly Ivanovich swore internally. 'And because of them, I'll have no holidays. What bizarre routines we're falling into. Almost every year there's something: one year it's the Olympic Games, then it's conferences, now this Festival ... They come here to make love. It's "Workers of the world, copulate!" This Festival's a farce! If only I could take my leave in September, at least I could go mushroom picking. But no! I'll get it around the new year . . .'

Vitaly Ivanovich pulled a face, stubbed out his cigarette in the ash-tray and went on with a sad smile: 'That's right, Olya, we're going to take a great interest in him. He comes here as the representative of a firm of chemical products, but he has links with the secret services, we know that for certain. In fact, for a time he was an expert on military affairs, but that's just for your information. We think he's going to make a contact. So it's not impossible that someone may pass documents to him. It would be very helpful for us to be able to examine his briefcase. Clearly that can only be done at night, you understand. Of course customs will go over him with a fine-tooth comb when he leaves. But before they get to customs they generally have time to encode it or learn it by heart or even entrust it to the diplomatic bag. So you see your role is crucial, Olya. He's due on the third of May and leaves on the seventh. He'll be staying at the Intourist.'

Olya passed on the German's smart black attaché case for inspection the very first night. It was an object of quality and price, like all the things this man used.

Olya waited until he was breathing regularly, and slipped out of bed. She knew he would sleep deeply for at least two or three hours. The sleeping draught was added to the cocktail. At the table in the restaurant, as if she had just happened to think of it, Olya would exclaim: 'Oh! I completely forgot! They do a cocktail here – you know, it's a rather . . . Russian style combination – absolutely delicious.'

If for any reason the 'subject' refused, the waiter would bring exceptionally salty caviar. In the bedroom, after the love play had left him breathless, the foreigner would take eager draughts of the cool wine thoughtfully poured out by his attentive companion.

Olya took a large black plastic envelope out of her bag, put the German's briefcase into it and closed the zip. Then she placed the envelope close to the door, gently withdrew the key from the lock and went over to the telephone. She dialled twice and, without waiting for the customary 'Hullo', murmured 'forty-six' and hung up. Two minutes later the lock clicked softly, the door opened slightly, and a hand deftly seized the black envelope. To avoid falling asleep, Olya did not lie down; she sat in an armchair.

Almendinger was lying on his back, stretched out fully, his great bony hands crossed on his chest. The neon light from the street silvered his face. It was a face that resembled a mournful plaster mask. And it now seemed impossible that the petrified folds of this mouth should, only a few minutes ago, have sought and touched her lips, those hands held her body.

During dinner at the restaurant he had talked a good deal, joking and correcting her mistakes. He bore himself with such worldly ease and there was such precision in all his words and gestures that Olya had no need to act. It felt as if he knew the scenario quite as well as her, that the allocation of roles suited him and in no way discomfited him. It even felt as if it was all so familiar to him that he was intent on making the most of this May evening, the presence of this young escort, as unexpected as she was inevitable, and of the chance, possibly for the last time in his life, to assume the rewarding role of social lion.

With smiling grace he talked about trips he had made, knowing that for his young companion the names of Venice or Naples had the same exotic ring as that of Eldorado. Generally in such recitals Olya used to detect a note of superiority, be it open or covert, on the part of those who lived on the other side of the Iron Curtain. Almendinger's stories were different. For example, in Italy he had for the first time in his life heard a cats' concert. A sadistic Neapolitan had gathered up a dozen cats, had arranged them according to their voices, putting them into tiny cages fitted inside a piano. He had inserted needles into the felt on the hammers so that every time the keys were struck they pricked the cats' tails. The wretched animals each emitted a different sound and their wailing blended into a horrible and pitiful symphony. The sadistic pianist had almost been lynched by the members of the local branch of the Society for the Prevention of Cruelty to Animals.

After telling this story Almendinger threw Olya a somewhat sheepish glance.

'I shouldn't be telling you about such horrible things. After all, we Germans have the reputation among you as a people somewhat lacking in humanity. Yes, that war ... When I think that in '41 I could see the Kremlin towers through my binoculars! And now I can see them from my bedroom window. It truly is as the Bible says: "*Die Wege Gottes sind unergründlich*". God's ways are unfathomable. Have you ever come across that expression?'

He fell silent, his gaze lost somewhere among the cups and plates. Remembering the part she had to play, Olya suggested with exaggerated animation: 'Oh, listen, Wilfried! I'd completely forgotten. They have an absolutely delicious cocktail here . . .'

Never before had these words seemed so loathsome to her. It was just at the moment when they brought the cocktail that he began to talk about the Germany of his childhood.

'You know, children these days have a great many toys. But all these toys are too cold, too ... how can I put it? Technological. When I was a child I had a collection of miniature lighthouses. The top of each one unscrewed and inside there was sand. Each contained a different kind of sand that came from a different beach in Europe . . .'

Almendinger lay there, his arms folded, his face motionless, now and then emitting a faint sigh, a brief moan.

He knew he would have to remain lying there like that for an hour, or perhaps two. He had heard Olya standing stock still above him, listening to his breathing, then telephoning. He had also heard the door open and close again. He rather regretted having chosen to remain stretched out on his back. On his side, with his face hidden in the pillow, it would have been easier. On the other hand, by slightly opening his eyes he could observe what was happening in the room. But even this was of little interest to him. Within his attache casé, a few pages of anodyne disinformation had been slipped with professional dexterity into the middle of a wad of scientific documents. This should smooth the path for his successor as he made a start in Moscow. What Almendinger was preparing to take away with him boiled down to four columns of figures learned by heart.

While he was talking about his childhood collection of lighthouses and their sand, he had been slowly bending the straw in his cocktail glass with his thumb. The glass stood behind the bottle of champagne and the carafe of water. Olya could not see it. He drew gently on the straw and slipped the end of it into an empty glass.

'And then,' Almendinger went on, 'my cloudless childhood came to an end, alas. I turned into a clumsy great oaf, a nasty little monster. One day I poured out all the sand into one small heap on the lawn. I mixed it all up.'

Olya, who was listening attentively and dreamily, asked in surprise in German: '*Warum?*'

Almendinger smiled. She suddenly seemed so young to him!

'*Und warum sind die Bananen krumm?*' he asked her, laughing. 'Why are bananas bent?' After that he remarked: 'This cocktail is quite excellent. I must remember its name. What did you say? "Moscow Bouquet"? Ah! A very good name for it . . .'

He put the straw to his lips. The last drops of delicate pink foam were disappearing from the bottom of the glass.

And now, lying there in the darkness of his bedroom, he reflected that everything in this world was strangely linked. That mixing of the sands had come back to him one night in a trench near Moscow. It was appallingly cold. The soldiers crowded round the stove. The red-hot metal burnt their hands, while their backs grew hard and stiff like bark under the piercing snow squalls. Above their heads the icy stars twinkled. And close by them, in similar trenches, crouched their enemies, the Russians. But these men, savages that they were, did not even have a stove.

'Tomorrow, or the day after tomorrow,' he was thinking, 'we'll be in Moscow. We'll have dealt with Russia. It'll be warm and clean. I'll get a medal . . .' A solitary flare went up, momentarily eclipsing the starry sky. Then their eyes had adjusted to the dark once more. And once more the stars began to shine and the deep black of the sky was restored. Trying to think of nothing, he reached out towards the stove, mentally repeating: 'Tomorrow we'll be in Moscow. It'll be warm, and clean . . .' But the thought he was trying to keep at bay returned. It returned not in words but as a vivid, instinctive flash: this snow-filled ditch dug out of the earth floating away into the dark of the night, among the stars. And all of them in this ditch, who have already seen death, who have already killed. And over there in a similar ditch, covered in hoar-frost, those whom they will have to kill. And this stove into which all the heat in the universe is concentrated that night. And the grains of sand from all the shores of Europe mixed up together in a little greyish mound on the lawn in a German town that has recently come to know the whistle of falling bombs . . .

In the bedroom the silence of the night reigned. Only from time to time the hiss of a car disappearing up Gorky Street and, apart from that, somewhere up on another floor, the short, sharp creak of a floorboard. From the Kremlin tower came the airborne melody of the chimes, then three solemn and measured strokes.

Olya was comfortable in her armchair. She observed the German as he slept and with difficulty restrained an incomprehensible impulse – to approach the bed on tiptoe and run her hand lightly over that plaster mask and bring it back to life.

Almendinger was automatically counting the vibrant strokes from the chiming clock in the tower: 'One, two, three. Three o'clock . . . They're spending a long time searching. They're testing it by radio, they're listening with a stethoscope. No, it's better not to think about it. Once you focus your mind on it for a minute you realize the totally phantasmagoric nature of everything around us. The night . . . and them. They've put their gloves on and now they're fingering, reading, taking photos. Red-eyed, yawning, their shirt sleeves rolled up. And I'm lying here, stupidly motionless. I, who forty years ago lay on the frozen earth, dreaming of warmth and rest in Moscow . . . And her. She's still so young; I have a daughter older than her. She sits there in her armchair, waiting for that idiotic briefcase. Absurd!'

Once more he remembered how, as a prisoner, he had been led through the streets of Moscow in that interminable column with other German prisoners. On both sides of the road, the people of Moscow stood on the pavement, staring at the grey tide of soldiers with somewhat wary curiosity. After them, following in their footsteps, came a slow-moving water cart, more or less symbolically washing the streets of the capital clean of the 'fascist plague'. It suddenly seemed to Almendinger that he was starting to picture the faces of the Muscovites standing in the street, to hear snatches of their conversation . . .

The door lock clicked softly. He realized he had fallen

asleep for a moment. Furtive footsteps glided over the carpet, the attaché case returned to its place beside the desk. As he fell asleep Almendinger felt the coolness of a light palm upon his face. But he was already so engulfed in his sleep that all he could do was to turn his face with closed eyes towards this hand, and smile, already dreaming, and murmur a few words in German.

By noon it was very hot in the colourful streets, awash with people and sunlight. You could already smell the summer, the scent of hot, dusty asphalt.

Ivan walked slowly along, dazed by the noise from the streets, the scorching sun, the red patches of the slogans, flags and banners. The words of the passers-by, the hooting of the cars and, above all, the blinding glare of the sun caused him acute pain. It seemed to him that it would only take a word, or a little laugh, and his head would explode. He tried not to look at the bustling pedestrians. He had an impulse to stop and shout at them: 'Shut up, won't you?' or to hit someone, so that for a moment, at least, the noise rending his brain might cease.

In his suit and raincoat he was horribly hot. He felt his shirt and trousers sticking to his skin, and his throat smarted from a dry tickle. But he walked on like an automaton, without taking off his raincoat, in the hope that at the next turning a cool breeze would at last be blowing and these noisy outbursts of merriment would fade away.

The night came back to him in confused snatches, with the hallucinatory insistence of that bare bulb on the ceiling. As soon as he began to remember, its light swelled, became ever brighter, ever harsher, and burned his eyes even more than the May sunshine. With his eyes half closed, Ivan pressed on.

He remembered how, after returning to Semyonov's room the night before, they had pulled out the suitcase with its store of alcohol from under the bed and begun to drink.

Ivan drank without saying a word, ferociously, constantly fixing Semyonov with his heavy, hate-filled stare. This look frightened Semyonov, who blurted out in a low voice: 'What do you expect, Vanya ... We've been taken for a ride like filthy pigs in a farmyard! Good God! They stuck all those medals on our chests and we, poor silly sods, were happy. Hero! Just you try showing your face in that bar where the Fritzes drink. They'll sweep you away with a yard broom. Even if you were a Hero three times over ...'

Then through the mists of the alcohol, no longer able to hear himself, Ivan was shouting something at Semyonov and thumping on the table with his fist. This thumping was suddenly echoed by a furious banging on the door and the shrill voice of the woman in the next room: 'Semyonov! I'm going to phone the militia. They'll take you away, you and your drunken mate! You're waking the whole house with your din ...'

Semyonov went out into the corridor to do some explaining. Ivan remained alone. There was complete silence now. From the ceiling the lemon-yellow bulb threw stark shadows: the bottles on the table, Semyonov's crutches at the head of the bed. Somewhere above the rooftops the strokes of three o'clock rang out ...

Coming towards Ivan were retired army officers who had put on their full dress uniforms in honour of the holiday. They were decked out in the armour-plating of their decorations. Ivan stared almost in horror at their swollen necks, their cheeks pink from shaving, their monumental torsos tightly swathed in belts and cross straps. From a gigantic banner a soldier, a sailor and an airman beamed formidable smiles beneath a fluorescent inscription: 'Long live the fortieth anniversary of the Great Victory!' Ivan wanted to stop and shout out: 'This is all rubbish. It's a fraud!' He'd have liked one of the passers-by to shove him, or insult him, or a fat army officer to puff out his scarlet neck and start spitting out something threatening at him. Oh, how he would have responded to them! Reminded them of how all these bloated ex-officers had been lurking to the rear of the lines, pointed out the American trade marks sported by the arrogant young whippersnappers walking past him.

But no one shoved him. On the contrary, at the sight of his Star shining on the lapel of his jacket, people stepped aside to let him pass. Indeed, when Ivan crossed the road where it was not allowed, the militiaman refrained from blowing his whistle, averted his head and looked the other way. With his energy flagging, Ivan turned down an alley and saw a cluster of trees at the bottom of it. But when he got to the end he found himself in a noisy and cheerfully animated avenue. Once again a vivid banner caught his eye: '1945–1985. Glory to the Victorious Soviet People!' Ivan stopped, screwed up his eyes and groaned. His brow and eyelids became damp, he felt weak at the knees. A water cart drove by, enveloping him in a smell of wet dust; a huge Intourist coach sailed past with smoked-glass windows, behind which well-groomed ladies with silvery hair could be seen. Ivan retraced his footsteps.

At that moment above the glass door of a shop he sensed, rather than read, in bulbous black lettering: 'Beriozka'. Without thinking, guided by an intuition about what would happen and anticipating it with spiteful glee, he went in.

A pleasant half-light prevailed in the shop. The cool temperature produced by the air-conditioning was disorientating. Lightly-clad tourists were talking among themselves beside a counter. A shower of shrill, discordant notes rang out, followed by a shout of laughter: one of them was buying a balalaika.

Ivan stopped near the counter. His gaze, scarcely taking objects in, slid over Palekh lacquer boxes, bottles of Scotch whisky, brightly-coloured album covers. Two sales assistants watched him attentively. Finally one of them, unable to hold back, said softly but very distinctly and without even looking in his direction: 'This shop, citizen, is reserved for foreign visitors. Payment here is made in currency.' And to show him that the conversation was at an end and that he had no more business there, she said to her colleague: 'I think those Swedes have made their choice. Wait here, I'll go and serve them.'

Ivan knew very well that it was a Beriozka. He also knew what a despicable peasant he was in the eyes of these two dolls in their elegant make-up. But that, precisely, was fine. Yes, it was fine that his head was exploding, his shirt sticking to his skin, that the foreigners – these extraterrestrials in their light T-shirts – should be buying things, laughing, their blue eyes staring through him into the distance.

'Go ahead, my girl. Go and serve them,' mocked Ivan. 'That's all we're good for. Serving them. Some in bed, some behind the counter . . .'

The sales assistant stopped, exchanged brief glances with her colleague and rapped out: 'I repeat: roubles are not accepted here. Vacate the premises or I'll call the militia. And take your hands off that glass case.' And in a lower voice she added: 'Any old country bumpkin thinks he can come in here. And then we have to wash the glass.'

Ivan clenched his teeth and leaned with all his weight on the glass of the counter. There was a sound of the glass breaking and at the same time the sales assistant's cry: 'Lyuda, call the duty militiaman!'

'You see these hands,' shouted Ivan. 'I loaded a whole mountain of shells into the guns with them. With these hands . . .'

He said nothing more and erupted into laughter like a barking dog. The agony tore at his eyes. But through the morass of his confusion suddenly everything became clear to him: 'All this is bullshit. To them I'm just a Neanderthal. Why am I telling them about those damned shells?' And, still laughing, he yelled out to the bemused foreigners: 'Now just you listen to me! I spilled gallons of blood for you, you bastards! I saved you from the brown plague, ha ha ha! . . .'

The militiaman came in. Thickset, a dull face, a damp red mark on his forehead left by his cap.

'Your papers, please, citizen.'

'Here are my papers.'

Ivan tapped on his Gold Star. There was a smear of blood on his raincoat. The palm of his hand had been cut by a fragment of glass.

The militiaman tried to grasp him by the elbow.

'You'll have to come to the station.'

Ivan jerked his arm free with a sudden movement. The militiaman stumbled; the crunch of glass could be heard beneath his shoes. The balalaika slipped from the grasp of one of the Swedes, who were watching the scene in amazement. It fell onto the marble paving and emitted a pitiful groan. Everyone was rooted to the spot in a mute, uncertain pose.

'Just a minute, Lyosha,' the sales assistant murmured to the militiaman. 'First let me show the foreign visitors out.'

At this moment two Japanese men came into the Beriozka, almost identically dressed. Had not one of them been slightly taller, they could have been taken for twins. Dark official suits, ties that glittered slightly.

Smiling, they walked up to the counter and, as if they noticed neither the broken glass, nor the militiaman, nor even the old man with a bloodied hand, they began speaking in melodious English. Pulling herself together, the sales assistant offered them a long, black leather case. Ivan stared at them, almost spellbound. He sensed that life, like duckweed displaced by a stone, was about to settle back into the well-ordered equilibrium that was so alien to him.

The Japanese, having made their purchase, headed for the exit; the militiaman took a step towards Ivan, crunching a fragment of glass underfoot. Then Ivan seized a statuette that was standing on the counter and hurled himself in pursuit of them. The Japanese turned. One of them had time to dodge the blow. The other, hit by Ivan, collapsed onto the paving.

Ivan lashed out blindly, without really managing to harm them. What was more alarming was his yell and his blood-stained raincoat. The Swedes scurried towards the door, yelping and pushing one another. As Ivan's fingers struck out, they knocked over a bronze figurine of a bear cub, an Olympic souvenir, which shattered the glass shopfront into fragments. Commemorative items of this kind had not sold well at the time of the Games; no one wanted to land themselves with such a burden. The whole series had been shipped out to the provinces: only this one had remained. The sales assistants kept it on the counter as a paperweight . . .

Almendinger came to the Beriozka shortly before closing time. He was glad he knew Moscow so well that he could make his way there not along Gorky Street but following little shady alleys. One of them pleased him particularly. It was quiet, almost deserted. You walked along beside the old brick building of a tobacco factory. Behind its walls could be heard the low, regular hum of machinery. The slightly bitter smell of tobacco hovered all along the alley.

'Little by little I'm going to forget it all,' thought Almendinger. 'All those figures, all those Moscow telephone numbers, all these winding alleys . . . And this smell, too. Now that's something to keep me busy until I die – forgetting . . .'

The side window at the Beriozka shop was cordoned off with a rope stretched between two chairs. The sales assistants were talking in whispers. All Almendinger could hear was: 'Mad . . . completely mad . . .' A glazier was at work behind the counter. Bowed over the table, he scored a long groove with his diamond, making a dry, grinding sound. Then, with a brief musical tinkling, he snapped the glass.

Almendinger smiled and asked the sales assistant to show

him a small gold watch for a woman. 'Or perhaps it would be better to buy a necklace or a bracelet, this silver one with amethysts and emeralds? Of course it would be much simpler to ask her what she would prefer. But what can you do? I'm getting old . . . It's tempting to play Santa Claus – or rather the Count of Monte Cristo of the third age . . .'

After a fine morning the sun was in hiding and the evening was grey but, as always at that time of year, luminous and strangely airy. On emerging, Almendinger turned left and entered a well-tended square in an open space with a rather provincial appearance. At the centre of the square a huge bronze column towered upwards, covered with a tracery of writing in Russian and Georgian – the monument in honour of the friendship between the two peoples. He sat down on a bench and, with a pleasure he could not quite understand, began watching the people and the long buses that drove round the square with weary dexterity. He caught gestures and snatches of conversation that were quite without significance for him and were for this reason utterly engaging.

Not far away there was a shoe shop. People came by with their cardboard boxes, still flushed from the pushing and shoving and the joy of purchase. A woman sat down on the edge of the bench beside him, took off her old down-at-heel pumps and put on those she had just bought. She turned her foot this way and that, studying it from all angles, then stood up, took a few paces on the spot – are they too narrow? – and made off for the bus. The toes of the old abandoned shoes were left sticking out from under the bench.

Almendinger realized he was still holding the little parcel from the Beriozka shop in his hand. He opened his briefcase and slipped his purchase into a small leather pocket. He saw the wads of paper there, the neatly arranged files, and smiled. A tipsy passer-by came up and asked him: 'Tell me, friend, you don't happen to have any matches, do you?'

Still smiling, Almendinger held out a lighter to him. When, after several attempts, the man managed to light his cigarette and mumbled: 'Thanks for coming to the rescue, friend,' and tried to return the lighter, Almendinger was no longer there. He was already strolling towards the alley that smelled of bitter tobacco.

Ivan remained in hospital for a long time, recovering from the heart attack he had suffered in the militia van. The inquiry took its course. No serious charges were brought against him. The Embassy sent a note to the Ministry of Foreign Affairs. An article appeared in a Swedish newspaper: 'Failed Hold-up in Moscow Beriozka Shop'. The following day 'Radio Liberty', broadcasting from Munich, gave the facts, mentioning the full names of all the participants correctly. Everyone knew that the story would soon evolve into one of those piquant anecdotes that are related at diplomatic cocktail parties: 'It actually happened at the Beriozka, you know. And a Hero of the Soviet Union, what's more! A Gold Star on his chest . . . Oh no, he's had his psychiatric assessment. A man of perfectly sound mind . . . You're right. Maybe it's what they call the Old Guard syndrome. Have you heard what that chap Petrov says about it? Quite priceless! He's meant to have stamped out all that kind of thing. When they told him about it he nodded and growled: "Yes, the Veterans stay young at heart for a long time . . ." And by the way, the Veteran's daughter . . . Yes, yes . . . And there's another quite fascinating detail . . .'

At the beginning of June Ivan was transferred into preventive detention. While he was in hospital Olya had been to see him every day. They did not have much to say to one another. Olya would produce the latest newspapers and fruit and food from her bag and ask after his health. Then they would go down and sit on a bench in front of a flower-bed that gave off the bitter smell of marigolds.

In the course of these two weeks, by borrowing money left and right and exchanging foreign currency, she settled accounts with the Beriozka. She telephoned Alexeï . . . It was sometimes his father, sometimes his mother who picked up the phone, and each time they replied politely that Alexeï was not there. His mother added: 'You know, Olyechka, he's preparing for the Youth Festival at the moment. He's gone to France to sort out some problems to do with the make-up of the delegation.' Olya thanked her and hung up.

Sometimes a longing overcame her, pathetic in its unreality: like a child who has broken a cup, she wanted to go back, to play the scene over again, so that the cup doesn't slip from her hands, so that there should not be this resounding and irremediable silence. But even this pathetic regret vanished.

With surprised incredulity, she saw that she was beginning to get used to a situation which, a little while previously, would have seemed to her inconceivable. She was getting used to this orange flower-bed, to this thin old man emerging from the dull fug of his room to meet her, to the inquisitive and merciless stares in the corridors of the Centre. And the fact that nothing had radically changed seemed to her disturbing.

It was very hot in Moscow at the end of May. Sometimes through the open windows of the Centre the long, slow siren of a ship could be heard, coming from the Moskva River. It even seemed as if you could smell the warm, muddy smell, the smell of the wet planks of the landing-stage in the heat of the sun. And when evening came the streetlamps already cast a blue light over the thick foliage, as they did in summer. In the restaurant, amid the dense aroma of spiced dishes and perfumes, the tinkling of a little spoon or a knife had an agreeably cool resonance.

Svetka consoled Olya as best she could. But she was so happy herself at that time that she went about it clumsily. A little while earlier, her Volodya had sent her a smiling photograph of himself and a letter in which he promised he would be coming home on leave for a whole month. In the photo two big stars could be seen very clearly on his epaulettes.

'So long as Gorbachev doesn't call it off in Afghanistan,' she commented, 'Volodya's sure to come back with his three colonel's stars. Of course, it's not much fun for him over there. But are things any better here? Apparently he's been in some garrison miles from anywhere for a long time, somewhere in Chukotka . . . Oh! I can't wait for August! We'll whizz off to the Crimea, we'll rent a little chalet by the sea. At least he'll get a proper tan. Last time he came back, you know, his face was like a Negro's, with just his teeth shining . . . and the rest of him all white!'

She checked herself, ashamed of her happiness.

'Listen, Olya, you mustn't worry. Your father, what can they accuse him of? Only a brawl and at a pinch they'll throw in that he was drunk. He'll get a year in the back of beyond, with a suspended sentence . . . And as for your diplomat, don't worry. With men it's always like that, you know. There are plenty more fish in the sea. Look, when he comes back, Volodya will introduce you to one of his friends from the regiment. And maybe your diplomat will come back to you anyway. Obviously his father and mother have turned him against you. But it'll all calm down and be forgotten. And if he doesn't come back, to hell with him! Listen, you remember Katyukha, who worked with the Americans? She married a type like that. And he got up her nose all the time. "You've got no aesthetic intuition," he used to say. "No grasp of style. You can't tell the difference between Bonnard and Vuillard." That whole artistic elite used to gather at their place, lounging about in armchairs, knocking back Veuve Clicquot and "telling the difference". . . . And you know, she's a plain, straightforward girl. One day she'd had enough of all these stuck-up art-historian bitches and blokes with shrill voices. They were talking about Picasso at the time. And suddenly she came out with this riddle, which is a real scream. "What's the difference between Picasso and the Queen of England?" It's a hoary old chestnut, of course. You must have heard it a hundred times. "Picasso only had one blue period in his life and the Queen has them once a month . . . On account of her blue blood!" You can just imagine the faces they pulled, all those intellectuals! Her husband exploded: "That's not only an obscenity – I'm used to that. It's sacrilege!" The idiots. They'd have done better to laugh instead of acting like constipated cows. Katyukha wouldn't put up with it. "They're just daubs, your Picasso!" she shouted. "He was a salesman, that's all. He got the message that there was a market for this kind of vomit – it's what you all like – so he vomited . . ." What a hullaballoo! The women all charge out into the corridor and get their mink coats mixed up. The men squeal: "It's the Attila Complex!" Her dear husband goes into hysterics . . . He's already opened divorce proceedings, the bastard. He was always lecturing her: "Life is an aesthetic act . . ." And all the time he was injecting himself against impotence. What an aesthete!'

They chattered on till dusk, as in the good old days. And, as in the old days, Ninka the Hungarian came to see them from time to time. She, too, set about consoling Olya, relating melancholy tales of her own life hitting the rocks many times, of disappointed hopes and other people's black ingratitude . . . But she, too, found it hard to conceal her own happiness: in June she was to make her last visit to the Black Sea coast. In October she would marry and would found what she herself laughingly called: 'a model Soviet family'.

Yes, everything remained as before. Nothing changed. Just one thing, perhaps. When she came home from work now she was vexed to notice that it was as if her face were covered by a sticky mask. She hastened to the bathroom to rid herself of it, scrubbing her cheeks. She tried to reassure herself. 'I'm running around like a madwoman at the moment. And in all this heat . . .' She remembered how after work Svetka always used to hurry to the bathroom, calling out to her, without stopping: 'Hang on, Olyechka. We'll have a word in a minute. Just let me put on a new face.'

Olya realized it was not just the tiredness and the heat she was talking about.

Prior to the summer holidays there was a great deal of work at the Centre. On occasion Olya did not return home for three days in a row. During the day she attended trade meetings and in the evening put on her usual performance at the restaurant. During these three days she had not had a single minute to go and see her father in hospital.

One morning, when she was able to get there, he was waiting with cheerful and nervous impatience. They took their places on their usual bench, in front of the flower-bed. Ivan lit a cigarette. Then, rapidly stubbing it out, he spoke in a low voice. When Olya heard these muted tones a shiver ran down her spine. She thought her father was going to ask her questions about her work, about her life or – worse still – try to justify himself. Ivan had something else to say.

'You know, Olyuch, it's a very good thing you've come today. Tomorrow they're giving me my discharge and transferring me into preventive detention. I want to hand something over to you. Keep it and hide it somewhere. I'm afraid they'll take it away from me when they search me.'

Ivan unclenched his fingers – in the hollow of his hand shone the Gold Star.

Olya returned home in a rickety, half-empty bus. It was travelling along the ring road. On one side could be seen the new concrete blocks of flats, stuck there amid churned-up clay. On the other side open fields, misted over with transparent greenery. Olya sat with her face turned towards the window, so that her tears should not be seen. She had begun crying when she opened her bag and caught sight of the Gold Star, right at the bottom, where normally either her keys or her lipstick would be hiding. 'This is still his life,' she thought with tender bitterness. 'He thinks there are still people around who remember that war long ago, all that comradeship at the front . . . They're all just like children. A whole generation of grown-up children who've been betrayed. I only hope he doesn't know anything about me! I just hope he doesn't!'

She was still crying as she climbed the stairs to the seventh floor. She did not want to take the lift for fear of meeting someone she knew. But when she got to the sixth floor she could already hear Svetka's laughter and merry shouts. 'Aha,' thought Olya. 'Ninka's there and they're having a good time.' And at once she felt a little comforted. She pictured them already bustling about her, cheering her up, putting the kettle on to boil. No doubt Ninka had come to say good-bye before setting off for the south. With her fund of stories she would be unstoppable. Olya turned the key and went in.

Svetka's bedroom door was wide open. Svetka was sitting on her bed screaming with horrible, sobbing laughter. Her swollen eyes, on which not the smallest trace of mascara was left, glittered wildly, madly. On the floor was a suitcase with several garments spilling out of it. Her shoes lay in two opposite corners of the room – as if one giant stride had left them there. Olya stopped on the threshold without trying to understand a word of this horrible howling because it was all too clear. She simply repeated like an incantation: 'Svetka . . . Svetka . . .'

Choking with tears, Svetka was silent for a moment. She sat there, with her eyes closed, her whole body shuddering, breathing jerkily and noisily. Cautiously Olya sat down beside her. Svetka felt her hand on her shoulder and began wailing in ever more desperate tones: 'Olka, a sealed zinc coffin . . . and you can see nothing . . . just his eyes, through the little glass

142

window . . . no eyelashes, no eyebrows . . . Maybe there's nothing there . . . in the coffin!'

And as she shook her head, she burst into tears once more. And once more, in a broken voice she cried out: 'A little glass window . . . And only his eyes . . . only his eyes . . . He's not there . . . No . . . Burned in the helicopter! There's nothing in that coffin. Nothing . . .'

Then, breaking free from Olya's arms, she jumped up and rushed to the wardrobe. She opened the door with a violent gesture and began pulling out boxes and cardboard cartons and throwing them on the floor.

'So who's going to make use of any of this stuff now?' she cried. 'Who?'

Out of the cardboard cartons tumbled men's shoes, brand new shiny boots made of first-rate leather; there were piles of shirts with Beriozka labels, jeans, ties. And, uttering a heavy sigh, Svetka collapsed in a heap on the bed and buried her head in the pillow.

Sitting beside her, Olya scarcely recognized her friend in this woman, now so crumpled and aged. She stroked her hand gently, murmuring: 'Don't cry, Svetka, don't cry. It'll be all right. It'll all come right in the end. Look, things are going badly for me, too, but I'm bearing up . . . I'm bearing up . . .'

Svetka was leaving from Kazan Station. She seemed completely calm now, simply screwing up her eyes, as if to avoid seeing the happy and excited crowd. Olya made her way along beside her, holding in her hand a big plastic bag into which Svetka had thrown everything that wouldn't go in her suitcase. The bag was a great weight. Heavily-burdened people came charging along, bumped into one another, colliding with their luggage. It felt to Olya as if the handles of the bag were slowly stretching and would tear. The crowd moved forward with painful slowness. Sweating faces, skullcaps on shaven heads, children whimpering . . .

The compartment was pervaded by a warm smell of thick dust.

'Oh, you haven't brought anything to drink on the journey,' Olya suddenly realized.

Svetka shook her head silently. Leaping down from the carriage, Olya weaved her way towards the buffet. In the queue in front of a long glass-fronted counter where there were piles of dried-up sausage sandwiches, hard-boiled eggs and hazelnut biscuits, she consulted her watch nervously.

When she got back to the platform with a bottle of warm lemonade and two biscuits in a little bag, she saw two red lights receding down the track into the distance in a hot grey mist. She stayed on the platform for a moment, then set the bottle and the bag down on a bench and headed towards the metro.

During one of those crazy days at the start of the summer, Olya realized that she was pregnant. She accepted the fact with dull and weary resignation. 'In fact there's nothing surprising about it,' she reflected on her return from the clinic. 'With all that pressure and fraught as I was . . . At a time like that you could end up producing twins and not notice . . .' At the Centre she asked for three days' break to have an abortion and get herself on her feet again.

She had counted the days and she knew it had happened at the beginning of May when, as she listened to that tall German with the attractive name, she had forgotten the role she was playing. And she knew it was not just a matter of forgetting either.

She arrived at the hospital two hours before the wards and clinics were due to open. In the stillness of the morning she walked round the pale yellow building, crossed the road and sat down on a bench in a little courtyard surrounded by old two-storeyed houses. At the windows there were flowers in pots and crudely painted earthenware statuettes. 'It's just like at home in Borissov,' she thought. The pale, watery sunlight gradually filled the courtyard, illuminating the entrance halls with their wooden staircases and causing a cat sitting on a little wobbly bench to blink its eyes. Later on, Olya would try to understand what had happened on that sun-drenched early morning. She looked at the pale flowers behind the windowpanes, the sandpit all pockmarked by the rain that had fallen in the night, the tufts of grass thrusting up through the trampled earth of the courtyard. She looked as if seeing all this for the first time. Even the ordinary grey soil mixed with sand was astonishingly present to her eyes, there before her, with its little stones, its twigs, its burnt matches. She suddenly felt a sharp and gripping tenderness for this new vision, this joyful and silent wonder. This vision was no longer hers. She could already feel it within herself as something separate from her, but at the same time close, pulsating, inseparable from her breathing and her own life . . . As if she were experiencing it almost physically. Her eyes followed the cat as it slowly crossed the courtyard, shaking its paws and arching its tail. Olya knew she was not the only one watching it and knew for whom she was silently murmuring: 'Oh, look at that pretty little pussy . . . Look at its lovely whiskers, its white tail, its little grey ears . . . Let's go and stroke it . . .'

The houses were beginning to wake up. People emerged from the hallways with a busy tread, hurrying towards the bus stop. Olya followed them. Arriving home, she went to bed without undressing and fell asleep at once. Towards evening she was woken by the strident screaming of the swifts. She stayed in bed for a long time, watching the dusk deepening outside the open window. Occasionally a woman's voice would ring out from high up on a balcony: 'Maxim, Katya, come in! How many times do I have to call you?'

And at once, echoing in reply, a shrill pair of voices: 'Oh please, Mum! Just five little minutes more!'

The swifts sped by, close to the window, with a rapid rustling of wings. It sounded as if someone were abruptly tearing a thin strip of silk. 'How simple everything is,' thought Olya. 'And no one understands it. They go charging along, pushing and shoving. They don't even have time to ask themselves "What's the point?" And yet everything's so simple. And I was going mad, too – Alyosha, the flat in Moscow, abroad . . . It's painful to think about it but I'd begun to hate his parents so violently it gave me nightmares. All the time I dreaded them persuading him not to marry me. I almost prayed for them to be killed in a car or a plane crash! How horrible!'

It was so silent in the purple dusk that the sizzling of potatoes in a frying pan could be heard through an open kitchen window. Olya thought about the one whose presence in the world she had so clearly felt that morning. And now she immersed herself with calm joy in the future needs of the child, its little clothes, feeding it. Without knowing why, she was sure she would have a boy. She knew she would call him Kolka, that she would live with him at Borissov, that she would find some dull, monotonous job there, and the monotony of the peaceful, grey days that lay ahead suddenly seemed to her an unspeakable blessing.

She pictured how he would learn about the life of his grandfather, Ivan, and her own life. What had seemed to them like the disastrous collapse of all their plans would pass into his childish mind like a fairytale, a kind of family legend: his heroic grandfather, who had suffered for the truth in his old age; his mother who had refused to live in Moscow, because the life they lead there is noisy, and dangerous even, on account of the crazy cars.

'For the moment I'll say nothing to my father,' she thought. 'After the court case, when he's well again, I'll tell him everything.'

Vitaly Ivanovich listened to Olya without interrupting. His silence slightly disconcerted her. She spoke calmly, striving to be logical and convincing. Vitaly Ivanovich kneaded his face with his hand, nodding his head, and from time to time threw her a twinkling and somewhat distant glance. Olya knew that from her very first words he had grasped everything she was about to tell him and was now patiently waiting for the conclusion of her speech. She uttered her final words in louder and more resolute tones: 'You know, Vitaly Ivanovich, perhaps this is my destiny. In the end we each have our cross to bear. For some it's Moscow, for others, Borissov . . .'

Olya thought he would be in a hurry to dissuade her, and start to reason with her in an amiable and friendly manner: 'Listen, this is just a whim, you'll get over it,' or, alternatively, remind her in a dry voice of her duty and her responsibilities. But he continued rubbing his face, nodded and said nothing. It was only when he heard her final words that he murmured: 'Yes, yes, destiny . . . destiny . . .' Then, lifting up his face with its reddened cheekbones, he said: 'It's been a crazy night, the telephone didn't stop ringing. I'm finding it hard to keep my eyes open. As soon as I sit down I fall asleep. I'm telling you this because, as you so aptly pointed out just now, we each have our cross to bear.'

He smiled, weary and absent-minded.

'When I was a student, you know, I did philosophy at first; it was only later I changed to law. I was, so to speak, looking for myself. It always seemed to me that something didn't quite hang together, that it wasn't . . . When I embarked on philosophy I thought I should be immersed at once in the unfathomable mysteries of existence. Very well, I open Aristotle and he argues as follows: Why – excuse me – does the urine of a man who's eaten onions smell of onion? And the pinnacle of all philosophical thought was Brezhnev's speech to the last historic Party Plenum. When you're young all that's very painful! Now, of course, it's ridiculous even to think about it. We had a professor, you know, a kind of last of the

Mohicans, one of the remaining ones who had qualified at St Petersburg University. And been in the camps under Stalin, of course. Young people love professors like this. So I ran to him.

'"Here's how it is, Igor Valerianovich. I'm in the middle of an intellectual crisis, a crisis as profound as that of bourgeois philosophy itself. Suppose I do law studies. I qualify and I set out to crush the Rostov *mafia* as an investigating magistrate, braving the gangsters' bullets . . ."

'And then, of course, I talk to him about destiny, about vocation, about the cross I have to bear. And this old philosopher went on listening and then said to me: "And you, distinguished young man, do you know the parable of the human cross?"

'"No," I told him. "Never heard of it."

'"Well, listen. A man was bearing his heavy cross. He bore it and bore it and in the end he started cursing God. Too heavy, this cross. It's cutting into his neck, crushing him, bowing him low over the earth. He can't stand it any longer. God heard his lamentations and took pity on him.

'"'Right,' he told him. 'Follow me, unhappy man.' He leads him to a vast pile of crosses.

'"'Behold. All these are human destinies, you see. Cast aside your own cross and choose another. Perhaps you'll find a lighter one.'

'"The man is overjoyed and begins trying them out. He puts one of them on his shoulder. 'No, too heavy. Heavier than mine.' And he takes up another one. He spends the whole day running around the mountain of crosses and doesn't manage to choose one. Heavy are the crosses humans bear. Finally, towards evening, he finds one.

'"'Here,' he says. 'This one is lighter than the rest. It's not a cross, it's a real delight.'

'"And God smiles.

148

'"'But that's your old cross, the one you cast aside this morning . . .'"

'And that's the story. I personally approve of the professor, of course. And in my heart of hearts I think, like Goethe, as perhaps you do now: "All theory's grey, my friend, and green the golden tree of life." Ah, well. But in practical terms this is what we'll do, Olya. When is your leave due? In October? We'll bring it forward to July. You'll have the time you need for reflection. To choose a lighter cross . . .'

Ivan's case came up at the beginning of July in the ugly little court building for the area, from which the Moskva River and the huge dockside warehouses could be seen. It was an old two-storeyed building, the staircases were worn and the courtrooms full of dust. In the dark corridor there was a whole row of doors, padded with black imitation leather. When one of them opened, dark shelves piled high with thick files could be glimpsed, a desk covered in papers and, in the corner, a kettle on an electric ring. Out in the noisy, sun-drenched streets it was difficult to imagine that just two steps away from there such a place could exist, drab and silent, with people making tea on electric rings in this somnolent semi-darkness.

At one o'clock in the afternoon Ivan was led into one of the courtrooms where shaky chairs were set out in untidy rows. On a little platform stood the desk for the judge and the assessors; fastened to the front of this desk was the emblem of the Soviet Union. Behind a wooden rail could be seen the bench for the accused. The rail had been marked by hundreds of hands: scratches, crosses, dates, initials . . . On each side of the judge's desk stood the rather smaller tables for the prosecutor and the defence lawyer.

At one o'clock in the afternoon Ivan walked into this courtroom escorted by two militiamen: three hours later he was carried out from it, dead.

The window in the courtroom was half open but no coolness could be felt. The sun shone, hot and unmoving. Swaying gently, the fluffy seeds from the poplar trees floated in through the windows.

During those three hours facts had been produced apparently connected with the trial but at the same time infinitely remote from it. There were a lot of people. Everyone wanted to know all the details. The air in the courtroom was heavy and stifling. Some people fanned themselves with newspapers; others, going through clumsy contortions, took off their jackets, causing the chairs to creak. Two women in the back row talked the whole time, listening neither to Ivan's replies, nor to the judge, nor to the witnesses. It was hard to understand why they had come there to waste their time in a Turkish bath like that.

The voices rang out dully, as if muffled by the lightly fluttering poplar down. One of the women assessors was allergic to these fluffy flakes. She was constantly blowing her nose, blinking her red eyes and thinking only one thing: let it end as quickly as possible! All her colleagues thought the same. The sun made people sleepy. Most of them were already getting ready to go on holiday, gleefully counting the days: just another week and then . . .

The judge, also a woman, had done too much sunbathing at her *dacha* the previous Sunday and beneath her severe suit she now felt a stinging pain on her shoulders. She, too, wanted to make an end of these proceedings, pronounce sentence – a year's suspended sentence, she thought – and, as soon as possible, on her return home, anoint her shoulders with soured cream. That was the advice of the assessor who was suffering from the poplar down. 'Perhaps it's not an allergy but 'flu,' the judge thought. 'You sometimes get it in summer.'

No one could quite remember at what moment the accused, Demidov, instead of the brief reply he was asked for, began talking very loudly, stammering, almost shouting. The judge tried to interrupt him, tapping on the desk with a pencil and saying in a deliberately formal voice: 'That has no relevance to your case.' Then she thought it was better to let the Veteran get it all off his chest – all the more so because she had received a telephone call from on high advising her to bring the matter to a quiet conclusion, not to be too zealous.

Ivan talked about the war, about Stalin, about the Victory. He stuttered a little, alarmed by the silence that arose between his words, trying to break through the dense sleepiness of the afternoon. For no good reason he mentioned the Bolshoï, Afghanistan (here the judge began tapping on the desk with her pencil again) and the one-legged Semyonov. People pricked up their ears at first, then relapsed into uncomprehending indifference. Gorbachev had already allowed all this to be discussed in the newspapers. The women looked at their watches and the men, anticipating the suspension of the hearing, fiddled with their cigarettes. The ones in the back row, as before, paid no attention to anyone and were whispering. The judge said something in the ear of the assessor next to her. The prosecutor, picking at his sleeves, was removing little pieces of fluff from them.

At length Ivan fell abruptly silent. He embraced the courtroom with a slightly mad look and, addressing no one in particular, cried out with an old man's hiss: 'You have turned my daughter into a prostitute!'

At that moment he caught Olya's eye. He no longer heard the hubbub arising from the public nor the judge's voice announcing that the hearing was suspended. He grasped that what had just occurred was something utterly monstrous, compared with which his drunkenness and the brawl at the Beriozka were but trifles. His daughter's face was hidden from him by someone getting up to go. He turned his gaze towards the windows and was astonished to see that the windowsill was gleaming in the sunlight with a strange iridescent glow.

Then this light swelled, became dazzling and painful and suddenly the sill turned black. Ivan sat down heavily and his head fell onto the wooden handrail, marked with old dates and unknown names.

It was with some difficulty that the van pulled clear of Moscow in mid-Festival, picked up speed, as if in relief, and plunged onto the motorway to Riazan. The driver and his colleague came from Riazan themselves. They did not know Moscow well and were apprehensive of running into the traffic police, who were in evidence at every crossroads on account of the Festival. But everything passed off all right.

Olya was seated in the dark interior of the van. With her lightly-shod foot she steadied the coffin draped in red cloth as it slithered about at each bend in the road. The van was open at the back and above the tailboard there was a bright rectangle of light. As they drove through Moscow there were glimpses, sometimes of a street Olya knew well, sometimes of a group of tourists in garish clothes. Coaches bearing the emblems of the Festival scurried up and down the streets and here and there one could often make out the white jackets and blue trousers of the interpreters. All this reminded Olya of the Olympic Games and that summer, now so long ago. Then open fields began to slip past in the rectangle of light, the grey motorway, the first villages.

Miraculously, after two days of fruitless searching, Olya had found this vehicle and succeeded in persuading the driver to take her. He had agreed simply because they were going in the same direction. Olya had given him almost all the money she had left.

Halfway there the driver turned off into a side road and stopped. The van doors slammed and his colleague's head appeared at the back above the tailboard.

'Not too shaken? We'll be there in an hour. Wait a bit;

we're just going to call in at a shop. Everywhere's dry in Moscow, you know, what with the Festival and all . . .'

Olya heard the footsteps moving off. In the sunny rectangle could be seen part of an *izba*, a fence, a garden in which an old woman was stooping down to pull something out of the ground. It was hot. Little rays of sunlight filtered in through the cracks. Somewhere in the distance a dog barked lazily.

Olya was convinced that at Borissov, once they learned of her arrival, everyone would rally round to arrange the funeral and find the musicians. She even imagined a procession of local dignitaries in their grotesque dark suits, the tinny grinding of the band, the condolences to which she would have to respond with meaningless set phrases.

But it all turned out differently. The driver and his colleague, sweating and panting in an exaggerated manner, let the coffin drop on the table and made off, after extracting another ten roubles from her, on account of it being on the third floor. Olya was left all alone facing this long red box, fearsome in its silence.

In the morning she went to the vehicle pool where her father had worked. She was received by the new boss in jeans that were baggy at the knees. Once he had grasped what this was about, he began talking rapidly, without letting her get a word in edgeways. All the vehicles were requisitioned for summer work at the *kolkhoz*, the only two remaining ones lacked wheels, and half the personnel were away on holiday. And, in self-justification, he showed her the deserted yard, spotted with black patches of oil, and a lorry into whose engine a dishevelled lad was plunged up to the waist. 'And in any case,' added the boss, 'we're operating a self-financing regime now.'

'But I'll pay,' Olya hastened to say, to calm him down. 'Just give me a vehicle and some men.'

'But I've just told you, I can't,' groaned the boss, spreading out his arms in a gesture of helplessness.

At the Military Committee the officer on duty asked her to fill in a form, then went off in search of orders on the far side of a padded door covered in glittering studs. On his return he opened the safe, took out the Hero's certificate and handed it to Olya.

'Now we're all square with you. As for the funeral, you'll have to apply to the Veterans' Council. It's not our responsibility.'

Olya took out the photo of her father on the certificate and examined it with astonishment. It was a young lad with a round, shaven head, almost an adolescent, looking out at her. 'He wasn't yet twenty,' she thought in sheer amazement. The courtyard at the Military Committee was empty and silent. There was just one lanky soldier sweeping an asphalt path. The dust arose in a light cloud and settled back in the same place.

At the Veterans' Council there was no one. A sheet of card dangled on the notice-board bearing faded red lettering:

'Veterans' Day Parade to mark the fortieth anniversary of the Victory will take place on 9 May at 10 a.m. Assemble in Lenin Square. The participation of all members of the Council is strictly compulsory.'

'It's the summer,' said the caretaker dreamily. 'In summer it's only by chance that anyone gets himself round here.'

The Party's District Committee also seemed to be deserted.

'He's gone off at the head of a commission inspecting the region,' said the female secretary. 'He won't be back tomorrow either. In any case it's nothing to do with the District Committee. You need to apply to his former place of work.'

The next day Olya went round the circuit again. She demanded, implored, tried to telephone Moscow. That evening she dreaded going home. It was already the fourth day of her ordeal with the red coffin. Coming into the room where it had been set down, she was afraid to breathe, afraid of detecting a smell and losing her sanity. At night the coffin appeared to her in a dream, not long and red, as it was, but small, luxurious, varnished and painted like a lacquered box from Palekh. She kept trying to put it into a left-luggage locker. But sometimes she forgot to dial the code, sometimes she was prevented by passers-by. In the end, unable to bear it any longer, she had decided to retrieve the contents and throw it away. She tried to open it, to separate its two halves, as one prises apart the two halves of a shellfish. And indeed the coffin suddenly resembled a finely-modelled black shell, covered in mucous varnish. When she finally managed to open this bivalve, breaking her nails in the process, what she found inside was the celluloid doll she had had as a child, staring at her with strangely alive and moist eyes, like those of a human being.

The following morning Olya went to the cemetery. There, in a tiny shack, behind the dilapidated church invaded by wild plants, sat three men, with dried fish and bread laid out on a sheet of newspaper. They were drinking.

They listened to her request and shook their heads in unison: 'No, no, not a chance! Coming here out of the blue like this. Tomorrow's Saturday. We finish an hour early today. Right? So, what do you think we are? Slaves? You might as well come on Sunday while you're about it. No, no! It's not possible!'

Olya did not go away. She understood that they were going through this routine so as to be paid more. The men went back to talking amongst themselves, casting oblique glances in her direction from time to time, and extracting fish bones stuck between their teeth. Finally one of them, as if taking pity, said to her: 'All right, my beauty. You give us a hundred roubles now and fifty roubles after and we'll do you a first-class burial.'

'How much?' asked Olya, dumbfounded, thinking she must have misheard.

'A hundred and fifty,' the man repeated. 'So what did you think? We're not going to do the job for the sake of your pretty blue eyes. Least of all on a Saturday! There are three of us. And we have to give something to the boss. And the driver. Suit yourself! But I'm making this offer out of the kindness of my heart.'

And with a sharp crunch he bit into a huge onion.

Olya had only ten roubles left. The men sat there taking their ease, interrupting one another, swopping remarks about the funeral of a local notable. The whole shed was cluttered up with frayed old wreaths, tombstones, and iron bars for railings. Olya had an impulse to say to these men in a low voice: 'For heaven's sake have pity on me, you bastards!'

'If I bring the money tomorrow morning,' she asked, 'is that all right for you?'

The men nodded their approval. 'Yes, that'll be fine. We'll start digging in the morning, before it hots up.'

When she got to Moscow Olya began telephoning all the people she knew, but reaching someone in summer and especially on a Friday evening was very difficult. The only one who responded to her call was a vague acquaintance, a dealer Ninka had introduced her to.

'Olya,' he exclaimed into the receiver almost joyfully. 'I've been completely cleaned out. Yes, the law caught me near the Beriozka with hot currency. And they emptied the flat as well. I'm skint. Otherwise, you know, I'd be very happy to help you but I haven't got a bean. Hang on. I'll give you the address of a mate of mine. He can change your currency. What? You haven't got any? Well then, bits and pieces of gold. Write this down. He's called Alik. Yes, he's from Azerbaijan, a good bloke. A bit unpredictable, that's all . . .'

She arrived at Alik's place late in the evening. When she showed him the emerald bracelet and two rings he began to laugh.

'And you waste my time for that? No, young lady, I work

seriously. Do you think I'd risk ending up cutting wood in the North for five grams?'

And he was already hustling her towards the exit along the dark corridor. Suddenly, as if remembering something, she opened her bag and took out the Gold Star.

'And that?'

'Have you got the certificate?'

Olya held it out to him.

'With the certificate I'll give you a hundred roubles.'

'I need a hundred and fifty,' said Olya in a weary voice.

'Well, come back another day,' Alik said flatly, opening the door.

Outside Olya went into a telephone booth. There was an immediate reply.

'Alyosha,' she whispered, almost without believing it.

'What a surprise!' a soft voice at the end of the line replied with quiet astonishment. 'Where have you been hiding? Well, you're right, it's my fault. I'm living between Moscow and Paris now. Our diplomatic clacking tongues have spread the word that you've been having some problems? Well, I'm sure it'll all sort itself out in the end. Do forgive me, I can't give you much time. I've got a meeting here with people responsible for the Festival. Yes, the French are here as well. It's a shame you can't come over. You'd be a charming flower at our all-male gathering. It'll all sort itself out in the end. Forgive me, I must get back to my guests now. Don't forget me. Give me a ring some time. And *bonne nuit!*'

Olya hung up. 'Diplomat!' she thought. Then took her lipstick and powder compact out of her bag.

When he opened the door Alik remarked to her carelessly: 'Ah! You've had second thoughts. And you were right to do so. A hundred roubles is a fair price. I'll have that Star on my hands for several months. There are not many collectors up for such a risk.'

'I need a hundred and fifty,' repeated Olya.

And she looked him in the eye for a long time. Alik took her by the elbow and in utterly changed tones observed: 'Hasn't anyone ever told you you have the eyes of a mountain deer?'

'Where must I go?' she asked in a weary voice.

The burial took place very quickly. The men worked swiftly and neatly. As they filled in the grave Olya noticed that dazzling dandelion flowers, cut by the spades, were falling into it, along with the earth, and this caused her a stab of pain.

By the afternoon she was sitting in the kitchen of her parents' flat. She stared at the walls which, before leaving for Moscow, her father had started to paint pale blue. On the gas stove the great old kettle that was familiar to her from childhood was hissing in a soothing manner. It seemed to her that everything was still possible; you just had to learn to stop thinking, to stop remembering.

At that moment a strident woman's voice rang out beneath the windows. 'Petrovna, they say there's butter at the Gastronom! Let's go there! We might get some.'

'So, how many packs does everyone get?' shouted Petrovna from her window.

But their voices were drowned by a man's bass voice: 'Don't be in a hurry, my little ladies. I've just been there. It's not butter. It's only good quality margarine. And there's none left anyway.'

Olya closed her eyes and for the first time in all these days she wept. She left for Moscow the same evening.

She spent much longer in the hospital than she had expected. After the abortion there were complications, then septicaemia developed. What saved her was a huge silvery poplar tree outside the window. Its leaves made a great rushing sound and filled the whole ward with their shimmering light, redolent of the sunny south.

* * *

The new client Olya was due to work with arrived at the beginning of October. Vincent Desnoyers, twenty-seven, deputy commercial director of an aeronautics firm. When he landed in Moscow a grey and rainy autumn was already beginning. The end of September, on the other hand, had been mild and serene, with morning frosts and warm, sunny afternoons.

During her first days out of hospital Olya took greedy breaths, unable to get her fill of the airy blue of the streets and the slightly bitter scent of the leaves. Close to the walls of buildings warmed in the sun the air was mellow and light, rippling densely in the purple shadows of the cool evenings.

The Centre continued with its customary busy life. The bronze cockerel was still regularly leaping about on its perch. The black wrought-iron figure of the naked Mercury on his pedestal was still running somewhere in the direction of the Moskva, brandishing his gilded wand. It seemed that all the trials and tribulations of the spring were left behind in the past. Few people at the Centre had noticed her absence. 'Did you have a good rest? Where were you? In the Crimea? In the Caucasus?' some people asked.

One day one of Olya's acquaintances caught up with her on the staircase, Salifou, a Guinean businessman. He had come to Moscow six years before and had concluded a contract to supply parrots to Soviet circuses and zoos. Since then, as it happened, he had long been handling major business deals but when they greeted him people never failed to remind him of this first contract.

'Hullo there, Salifou! Are your parrots still selling well?'

'Hopelessly! You're ruining me with the competition. Soviet parrots are the best in the world . . .'

Salifou showed Olya a photo.

'Here, I must show you my latest little one.'

She saw a young woman in flowery clothes, a baby in her arms, staring at the lens with an assiduous but at the same time half-sleepy air. To her left could be seen the shapes of a tree with dense foliage and a strip of blue-grey sky.

Olya studied the photograph and could not take her eyes off the young woman's face. In the calm, distracted gaze of her dark eyes, in the curve of the arm supporting the child, she sensed something that was intimately close and familiar to her. Olya understood that she should say a few words, offer an appropriate compliment. But she continued to stare, fascinated. Finally, without thinking, without detaching her gaze, she said: 'It must be very hot there, in your country.'

Salifou laughed.

'Of course! Like a Russian bath . . . Come and see us. You'll tan as brown as me, I promise you.'

And, slipping the photo back into his wallet, he went on down the stairs.

Olya put the Frenchman's briefcase into the big black envelope, slipped his address book into an inside pocket and placed the envelope near the door.

In the room a comfortable, somewhat sugary warmth prevailed. The Frenchman slept, the covers thrown aside, his arms wide outstretched. The paler skin about his loins made a striking contrast with the dark colour of his tan.

During dinner he had talked a good deal. And all his remarks were well judged, they all produced the smile, the look, the reply he had expected from his companion. He was in that agreeable state of mind where you feel that everything about you is sparkling, when you have the impulse to say to yourself: 'This young man, in his expensive, highly-fashionable jacket, his dark trousers with turn-ups, his luxurious golden-brown leather shoes – is me.' His well-groomed hair falls over his brow in a black fan. Nonchalantly, but fine-tuned almost to the millimetre, the knot in his tie is loosened. Even his cigarette smoke coils elegantly.

He talked a good deal and felt he was pleasing this woman.

He experienced this *joie de vivre* almost physically. The suave flavour of it was something he relished tasting. As he drank the cocktail he began talking about Gorbachev. Before leaving France he had read an article in *Libération* about the reforms in the USSR. It was all very well explained: why Gorbachev would never succeed in democratizing the regime, restructuring the economy, catching up with the West in the field of electronics.

'All the same,' he argued nonchalantly, as he sipped his cocktail, 'Russia is the land of paradoxes. Who was it began all these shenanigans with *perestroika*? A disciple of Andropov. In France they even call Gorbachev the "young Andropovian". The KGB as the initiator of democratization and transparency? It's science fiction!'

'I wonder where he is now,' thought Olya. 'That German with his collection of little lighthouses.'

As he was falling asleep, his thoughts racing, Vincent was considering what he could do to stay in Moscow for one more day or, more precisely, one more night. Telephone his boss and tell him he had not had time to sort out all the details of the prices? No, the old fox would twig straightaway. You couldn't pull the wool over his eyes. Maybe a problem with the plane? There were no seats left? Complications at customs? Yes, that's true, but then there would be the hotel. He would have to fork out for that himself. And then maybe he would have to pay her, this girl, or give her a present. How does that work? Anyway, it's not a problem. Some trinkets from the Beriozka should do the trick . . .

Sleep swept in abruptly. All at once everything that was on his mind began to be swiftly resolved, all on its own. He saw his boss talking to him amicably, walking with him along endless streets, half Muscovite, half Parisian. He extracted wads of notes from the cash dispenser that was actually located in the hotel bedroom . . . And once again, already dreaming, savoured in his mouth the sweet taste of happiness . . .

Olya put the briefcase back in its place, carefully slipped the address book, the right way round, into the inside pocket of the jacket. The silence in the room seemed to her strangely profound, unaccustomed. 'Perhaps it's because we're at the Rossia Hotel instead of the Intourist,' she thought. 'There's less traffic.' She went over to the window, drew back the curtain and suppressed an 'Oh' of surprise.

The first snow was falling. The trees covered in snow, the cars all white alongside the pavements . . . Olya could not resist and half opened the narrow, lateral fanlight. The first gust was difficult to breathe in – so sharp was this vertiginous scent of winter. 'It's good that the snow's falling,' thought Olya. 'When it freezes I'll go to Borissov, to the cemetery.' And she pictured herself – feeling no longer grief, but a calm bitterness, lodged somewhere beneath her heart – a grey winter's day; the frozen earth crunching underfoot on the pathway between each set of railings, the trees bare and the two graves, covered in snow and the last of the leaves, no longer frightening to her, maintaining their unimaginable watchful silence beneath the pale winter sky.

Only the Moskva River was black. And above it, on all sides, swirling up into the sky, or hanging motionless in the air, fluttered a white veil. All at once the muted sound of bells trembled within these snowy, icy depths. It was not the Kremlin clock but a thin and distant chime. It rang out from the belfry of a little church lost in all this silent snow, somewhere near Taganka Square. 'We each have our cross . . .' Olya remembered. And she smiled. 'And each our first snow . . .'

She shut the window, drew close to the bed and looked at the Frenchman as he slept. 'Without his clothes he looks like a boy,' she told herself. 'I must have chilled him opening that window.' Cautiously she drew the covers over him and slipped in beside him. Slowly, a little stiffly, she stretched out on her back.

Abruptly everything began to spin before her eyes – snatches of conversation, the sensation on her lips of all the smiling done that day, the people, the faces . . . the faces . . . Just before she drifted off, in the manner of a half-whispered childish prayer, a thought brushed against her. 'It would be good if he paid me in currency . . . I could buy back my father's Star . . .'

ANDREÏ MAKINE

A Life's Music

In a snowbound railway station deep in the Soviet Union, a stranded passenger comes across an old man playing the piano in the dark, silent tears rolling down his cheeks. Once on the train to Moscow he begins to tell his story: a tale of loss, love and survival that movingly illustrates the strength of human resilience.

'Masterly'
Paul Bailey, Books of the Year, *Independent*

'This year brought a number of good works of fiction. It also brought one great one . . . At the close, one feels that one has read not a novella but an epic.'
Francis King, Books of the Year, *Spectator*

'A masterpiece . . . A novella to be read in a lunch hour and remembered for ever'
Jilly Cooper, Books of the Year, *Sunday Telegraph*

'[It] has everything a Russian novel should have: truth, beauty, struggle and redemption, but without the bewildering patronymics or the excessive length.'
Toby Clements, Books of the Year, *Daily Telegraph*

'Beautifully laconic'
Max Hastings, Books of the Year, *Sunday Telegraph*

'Makine here is as good as Stendhal – or Tolstoy . . . Makine is storyteller, teacher, and enchanter most of all. I would rather read him than anyone else now writing, and then reread him. I think this is his best book so far.'
Allan Massie, *Literary Review*

'A masterpiece . . . both a page-turning adventure story and a parable.'
Ron Butlin, *Sunday Herald*

'Characteristically exquisite . . . Here is a haunting performance as assured and self-contained as a Chopin nocturne – to be enjoyed and remembered.'
Eileen Battersby, *Irish Times*

S

SCEPTRE

ANDREÏ MAKINE

Requiem for the East

Amid the ashes of the Soviet Union a Russian army doctor turned spy addresses the woman he loves – a fellow spy who has shared his shadowy life in Africa, Europe and the Middle East, but who has disappeared. The tale he unfolds spans three generations of his family, ordinary people caught up in the convulsions of the Russian empire in the twentieth century, from the civil war through the Second World War to beyond the fall of communism. It is a tale of brutality and soured dreams yet also one of heroism, tenderness and immense courage, written by a master.

'Andreï Makine has been compared to Nabokov, Chekhov, Proust. Far from flattering him, such plaudits barely begin to do him justice' Sam Phipps, *Spectator*

'There's no author writing today I admire more than Makine. This novel is extraordinary' Allan Massie, *Scotsman*

'An awesome achievement, head and shoulders above any novel that I have read so far this year.' Frances King, *Literary Review*

'As well as being a war story, each of the three lives carries a graceful love story, too, and each contrives an elegiac ending. At times, Makine's eye for the telling detail of battle or the first stirring of romance is reminiscent of Michael Ondaatje . . . By intimate accumulation of detail, he gives that history a resolutely human face' Tim Adams, *Observer*

'A powerful, passionate piece, epic in scope . . . His heart-felt portrait of everyday life in Russia is the best possible antidote to political oversimplification.' David Robson, *Sunday Telegraph*

'Makine's genius, made more evident with each strange and compelling new novel that appears in English, is in his ability to tune narrative to the underlying harmonies in the cacophony of displaced and mutilated lives . . . it is through [this] that this prodigiously gifted Russian novelist . . . creates a serene, redemptive music.' Rachel Polonsky, *Evening Standard*

SCEPTRE

ANDREÏ MAKINE

Confessions of a Lapsed Standard-Bearer

'An evocation of a Russian childhood in a little town near
Leningrad after the war. Alyosha, the narrator, and his friend
Arkady march joyfully through the forests, leading their
Young Pioneer troop with drum and trumpet towards the
"radiant horizon" in which they have been taught to believe.
They do not know about the watchtowers and prison camps
behind the trees . . . Then one day . . . the blinkers start to fall
from their eyes . . . Alyosha finally leaves Russia for Paris and
becomes a writer, while Arkady goes to America and prospers.
Alyosha feels they have both betrayed their childhood and
all it meant to them. But in this book, with its wonderfully
sharp, sensuous imagery and delicate delineation of feeling,
that childhood comes alive again. It is a moving and
gripping story' Derwent May, *The Times*

'A glory and a dream' Gary Atkinson, *Glasgow Herald*

'A beautiful piece of work . . . Makine has Chekhov's tender
humanity and wonderful ability to evoke states of feeling
by description of weather, landscape, buildings, etc . . . He
cannot fail to arouse in the reader a wistful nostalgia. There
is beauty in the world he makes for us, beauty and courage
and goodness flowering, despite the harsh wintry reality
of deprivation. His is a superb achievement . . . He is a
wonderful writer . . . You will be lucky if you happen upon a
better book than this' Allan Massie, Scotsman

'Stunning . . . the lasting impression from this excellent novel
is one of hope' Sam Phipps, *Scotland on Sunday*

'I am hard-pressed to think of another novel which captures
the essence of the old Soviet Union with such telling
economy . . . Makine is a master word-painter and, even in
translation, you can admire his precise brush work. It is less
than 150 pages long, but it has the panoramic sweep of the
great Russian novels of the nineteenth century'
David Robson, *Sunday Telegraph*

'[Makine] writes lyrically, with an intensity that appeals to all
our senses. He is adept at evoking both the everyday and the
extraordinary' Robert Chandler, *Independent*

SCEPTRE